MERRIMEN

JENNA
MADDY

<u>Jenna St. James Books</u>

Ryli Sinclair Mystery Series (cozy)
Picture Perfect Murder *Bachelorettes and Bodies*
Girls' Night Out Murder *Rings, Veils, and Murder*
Old-Fashioned Murder *Next Stop Murder*
Bed, Breakfast & Murder *Gold, Frankincense & a Merry Murder*
Veiled in Murder *Heartache, Hustle, & Homicide*

Sullivan Sisters Mystery Series (cozy)
Murder on the Vine *Tea Leaves, Jealousy, & Murder*
Burning Hot Murder *Flames, Frames, & Murder*
PrePEAR to Die

Copper Cove Mystery Series (cozy)
Seaside & Homicide
Merriment & Murder

A Witch in Time Series (paranormal)
Time After Time
Runaway Bride Time (novella)
Toy Time Tragedy (novella)

A Trinity Falls Series (romantic comedy)
Blazing Trouble
Cougar Trouble

Chapter 1

"I think we're ready for the party," I said to my two best friends, Peyton Patterson and Raven Masters.

"I love all the colors," Raven said.

Says the girl who only wears black.

Peyton looped her arm around mine. "I'm a little sad, though."

"Why?" I asked. "Aunt Aggie coming back is a great thing."

After nearly thirty years of being estranged from my Grams, my great-Aunt Aggie finally decided to move back to Copper Cove and make a new start. She and Grams were still finding their footing with each other, but after a month together, they seemed to be doing all right. Aunt Aggie had purchased the Bed and Breakfast across the street from where Grams and I lived, and tonight was the big grand opening for the town.

Peyton rested her head on my shoulder. "It's not your Aunt Aggie I'm sad about. Do you realize this might very well be our last Christmas together? We're seniors. From here on out, who knows where our lives will take us?"

Meow!

I swallowed past the sudden lump in my throat and bent down to pick up Jinx, my older-than-dirt black cat. "Don't say that, Peyton. We'll always be together."

Peyton and I had been best friends since kindergarten. We were both sort of outsiders in town. She was not only

3

super brainy, but model gorgeous. A dichotomy that confused most kids our age. The fact her dad owned the funeral home and was the town coroner didn't help matters, either. I was an outsider for different reasons. My mom abandoned me the first chance she got, giving me to my Grams to raise. That probably wouldn't be so bad on its own, but most townspeople thought my Grams was a witch because she owned the apothecary in town. Those were two big strikes against me.

Raven tossed back her purple hair. "Well, I think this is going to be *my* best Christmas ever."

Raven had moved to town at the beginning of the school year. At first I didn't really like her because she was so weird. She had purple hair, a nose ring, and she always wore black. Not the kind of girl I'd normally hang out with. That is, until I got to know her. When Granny Winnie had been accused of murdering two people last month, Raven was instrumental in helping us find clues to solve that mystery and keep Grams out of prison.

"There you girls are." Aunt Aggie strolled into the spacious great room...her hip-hugging designer jeans and pink-tipped white hair a stark contrast to her sixty years. "I was wondering—oh." She stopped and gazed around the room we'd just finished decorating. "This is gorgeous. You girls did a great job."

A skinny red and gold tree sat in one of the corners, lighted garland framed the fireplace, and we'd replaced her regular decorative pillows on the two couches with velvet jewel-colored pillows that had cute Christmas sayings.

"This is the last room," I said. "We've decorated the great room, front parlor, dining room, the downstairs bathroom, the library, and the—what's that fancy word you used to describe the room off the back of the house?"

"The conservatory," Aunt Aggie said.

I snickered. "Conservatory."

Aunt Aggie threw back her head and laughed, her spikey pink tips swaying with the movement. "You can call it a sunroom."

"Whatever it's called," Raven said, "it's decorated too."

"That's every room on the first floor except for your private bedroom area which is blocked off," I said. "And the kitchen."

Aunt Aggie nodded. "Chef Granger said he didn't want anything hindering his movements, so all Christmas kitchen décor had to be eliminated."

We followed Aunt Aggie back into the dining room where Grams and Henley Waller were sitting at the long table drinking coffee.

"I'm already exhausted." Grams snatched a gingerbread man from a platter and dipped it in her coffee before biting off the head.

I rolled my eyes. "You've been sipping coffee, eating cookies, and bossing us around all day. How can you be tired?"

"That's hard work," Grams said around a mouthful of cookie.

Mr. Waller gave me a wink. He lived a couple hundred yards up the road at the lighthouse. He'd been the lightkeeper for over thirty years—clear back when my Papa had been alive. The two men had even been best friends. Recently, Mr. Waller confessed to Grams he'd had feelings for her all these years. They've pretty much been inseparable the last month now.

Aunt Aggie glanced at her watch. "Chef Granger should be here any minute."

"I still can't believe you got Chef James Granger to cater," Raven said. "He's like the hottest chef around right now."

I scrunched up my face. "Uh...he's like the only chef around these parts. Copper Cove isn't exactly a metropolis."

Which is exactly why Grams and I spent a lot of our time fighting. I wanted to go away to college when I graduated in May, and she wanted me to stay in Copper Cove and work in her apothecary selling my soaps and natural beauty products. But the town only had nine thousand people...there was no way I was going to make a living selling beauty products. Plus, I just needed more.

Copper Cove sat along the natural cove of the Pacific Ocean in Mendocino County. Like a lot of coastal towns, the houses and storefronts were bright and cheerful and the townspeople were friendly and gossipy. And while I loved being able to look out my bedroom window and watch the boats and whales go by, deep down I knew it wouldn't be enough to make me truly happy.

"His restaurant is amazing," Raven said. "The food is delicious, and the staff is really nice. Sometimes he'll come out of the back and walk around and talk to people."

"It's weird you know him that well," I said.

6

Raven shrugged. "What can I say? Both parents are lawyers. We do a lot of eating out."

According to Raven, this Chef Granger was the ultimate when it came to anything food related. Two years ago he went on one of those reality cooking shows and won first place. Then out of the blue last year, he opened a restaurant on the outskirts of town between Copper Cove and the tiny town of Gillway. Since Grams cooked most of our meals, and we rarely ate out, I'd never been to his restaurant. But according to Raven, it was mega popular.

How in the world Aunt Aggie convinced this chef guy to come here and cook for the open house was beyond me. Supposedly it takes weeks just to get a table in his restaurant. Why would he want to come here and make little snack foods?

Meow! Meow!

"What's that, Jinx?" I asked. "Someone's here?"

"That's just freaky," Aunt Aggie said.

I don't know how or why, but for some reason, Jinx and I have always had this crazy connection. I swear I can understand what he says. No one was really sure where Jinx came from. Grams claimed he showed up on her doorstep the day my mom abandoned me.

The sudden pounding on the door had Aunt Aggie's eyes going wide. "See! Freaky!"

I chuckled. "Why's it freaky?"

"It just is," Aunt Aggie said as she strolled out of the dining room toward the front door.

"I think it's cool," Raven said.

I gave her a get-real stare.

She threw her hands up and laughed. "Okay. I admit I was a little freaked out the first couple times you did it."

I was about to tease her more, but Aunt Aggie's flushed face appeared in the doorway. Towering over her was a handsome man with silver hair flowing down to his shoulders. He had the palest blue eyes I'd ever seen, and a silver and black goatee. I wasn't good at guessing older people's ages, but if I had to guess, I'd say he was around Aunt Aggie's age. About sixty.

"Everyone, this is Chef James Granger." Aunt Aggie stepped aside and motioned to the man. "He and some of his staff are catering tonight."

Three women in black t-shirts proclaiming Granger Kitchen Staff in red glitter smiled and nodded.

Chef Granger gave a slight bow then turned to the group of women behind him. "Ms. Quinn has informed you where the kitchen is. Please begin preparing. I'll be along shortly."

Aunt Aggie smiled. "Call me Aggie, James. It's been a long time, but not so long you can't call me by my first name."

Whoa! What?

"You two know each other?" Raven asked, her voice filled with awe.

Chef Granger winked at Aunt Aggie. "Aggie and I go way back. Almost back to our diapers."

Aunt Aggie tittered. "Not quite that far. James and I were in the same class in school until he moved away our sophomore year."

8

"Jimmy Granger?" Grams stood up and hugged the handsome chef. "I don't know why I didn't put that together. I'm sorry for not getting out to your restaurant. Brynn and I don't really eat out a lot."

Chef Granger patted Grams' hand. "That's no problem, Winnifred. It's been a long time."

"You can call me Winnie," Grams said. "Everyone does."

"Do you remember Henley Waller?" Aunt Aggie asked.

The two men shook hands.

"Nice to see you after all this time," Henley said. "And I'm a lot like Winnie. No point going out to eat when you're used to eating for just one."

I grinned. "Now that you two are—what did they call it in your day—courting? Now that you two are courting, maybe you can go out on a date at his fancy restaurant?"

Grams narrowed her eyes. "I got me some cilantro in the refrigerator across the street, Brynn. Don't make me use it."

Chef Granger grinned at me. "Tastes like soap to you?"

"Yep," I said.

"So that makes you Brynn?" he asked.

"Yep," I repeated.

Raven stuck out her hand. "My name's Raven Masters, Chef Granger. Mom, Dad, and I eat at your restaurant at least once a week. We love it."

He gave her a wolfish grin as he shook her hand. "I thought I recognized you. And thank you, Miss Raven. I appreciate the praise."

Peyton gave him a small wave. "I'm Peyton, and I come from a large family. Mom pretty much does all our cooking.

But I did watch you on *Chefs Last Stand*, and you were by far my favorite. I was so excited when you won." Her brow furrowed. "They said you were from San Francisco on the show."

Chef Granger nodded. "I moved there when I was in high school."

"And you decided to move back *here*?" I asked. "And open a fancy restaurant? Why?"

Chef Granger cocked his head. "Why not? Copper Cove is a great place to live."

"But it's...*Copper Cove!*" I exclaimed. "You could have made bank in the city. Plus all the nightlife and entertainment." I sighed. "I can't wait to experience it for myself."

Chef Granger grunted. "You may come to change your mind on that, young lady."

I shook my head emphatically. "Never."

CHAPTER 2

"You girls look beautiful," Grams said as Peyton, Raven, and I walked down her staircase an hour later. "Look at you, Raven! In a color other than black."

Raven grinned. "I decided to throw caution to the wind and go all out for Christmas."

I snickered. "It's deep *purple*. Looks almost black."

"But it's not," Raven pointed out. "And that's all that matters."

All three of us had decided on different colored long-sleeved sweater dresses with ankle boots. Not what we usually wore to school, but since we were officially on Christmas break as of yesterday, it was time to get into the holiday spirit.

Meow! Meow!

I looked down at Jinx and laughed. "Grams, are you making him wear a bowtie to the party?"

"Yep. Just a tasteful red one."

Meow! Meow! Hissss!

Peyton laughed. "No need to translate what that meant. Jinx obviously isn't happy."

I looked out the front window of the house and saw the twins, Jessica and Janice, walking up Aunt Aggie's sidewalk. Jessica and Janice owned Sisters Bakery and Coffee Shop...one of my favorite hangouts in town.

"The twins and other guests are starting to arrive," I said. "We need to get across the street to help greet."

"Go ahead," Gram said. "Jinx and I will be along shortly. Henley is walking me over."

With a quick wave, the three of us scrambled outside and hurried over to Aunt Aggie's bed and breakfast. The outside was decorated just as elaborately as the inside. Big, white bulbs outlined all three floors of the house, and lighted garland spanned the wraparound railing.

I turned around to look past our house and out at the Pacific Ocean. It was too dark to really see the churning water, but I could hear the waves as they collided against the rocks and crashed onto the shore.

"C'mon." Raven tugged on my arm. "It's cold out here."

The party didn't officially start until seven, but tons of guests were already mingling inside by six-forty. I waved to Aunt Aggie but followed Raven and Peyton over to the twins. They were dressed in matching silver glittery dresses.

"Those dresses are killer," I said. "Love the glitter."

Jessica smiled. "Thanks. You girls looks adorable in your matching dresses too."

"And those boots!" Janice exclaimed.

"Two are the same color as our caramel macchiato," Jessica said, "and the other is a deep mocha."

I snickered. "Only you would describe boot colors in coffee flavors."

"Speaking of coffee," Peyton said, "I saw where you guys are looking to hire someone for deliveries."

I clapped my hands. "I'm so excited for that! Now I can have my fix whenever I want."

Janice smiled. "It's mostly evenings and weekends we'll need the help. I've decided to expand the menu and serve gourmet sandwiches on artisan breads, and I'm also going to have a soup-of-the-day available."

"We even bought the most adorable little Smart car and put our logo on it," Jessica added.

"If we know of anyone," I said, "we'll send them your way."

"You girls are the best," Jessica said.

"Who decorated?" Janice asked.

"We did," Raven said. "Looks good, right?"

"Beautiful," the twins said simultaneously.

Peyton, Raven, and I said goodbye and headed for the dining room, and straight to the tray of iced sugar cookies on the table. Snatching one up, I shoved it in my mouth and moaned. It was just the right consistency of soft cookie but hard icing.

"Are you eating the party food already?" Aunt Aggie joked.

I quickly swallowed and grinned. "Delicious."

She winked. "I've already had three. James says if he catches me again, I'm banned from the dining room."

We all jumped at the unmistakable sound of a tray crashing to the floor. A few seconds later, Chef Granger let out a string of curses. The four of us ran to the kitchen entryway—or the entryway from the dining room. There were actually two entrances into the kitchen.

"Is this how we're going to start the evening, Mariah?" Chef Granger asked.

"Sorry Chef," Mariah said. "It won't happen again."

He frowned at her for a few more seconds. "You got this. If she shows up tonight, you ignore her and carry on."

"Yes, sir."

The girl grabbed another tray of champagne and headed out the other doorway. Chef Granger grumbled to himself as he bent down to pick up the plastic flutes littering the ground.

"Let me get you a mop," Aunt Aggie said.

He looked up and scowled. "Usually Mariah isn't this clumsy. She's one of my best servers." He stood and took the mop from Aunt Aggie's hand. "About four months ago she and her fiancée broke up." He snorted. "Or I should say the fiancée's mother demanded they split up. Seems she didn't think Mariah was good enough for her son. Mariah's still trying to get over it."

"And you think this mean woman will be here tonight?" I asked.

"There's a good chance," Chef Granger said. "This is a pretty big deal to the community, and she's all about being seen in public."

"Who is it?" Peyton asked.

"Temperance Clairmont," Chef Granger said.

I gasped. "She's like the meanest woman in town."

"That she is," Chef Granger agreed.

"Can we help you do anything tonight?" Peyton asked.

Chef Granger finished mopping up the champagne and handed the mop back to Aunt Aggie. "Maybe. How about you come and check every half hour or so to see if anything needs replenished in the dining room. I'm having the servers pass out the hors d'oeuvres and the champagne. The coffee and desserts will be in the dining room. If you girls could check in on those throughout the night, I'd appreciate it."

"We can do that," Raven said.

"The extra cookies will be in the butler's pantry," Chef Granger said. "I want the counter space in here for the hors d'oeuvres."

I thought the butler's pantry was one of the coolest rooms in the house. In between the kitchen and the dining room, before you reached the entryway, there was a white pocket door. Inside was like a second kitchen. Lining three walls were countertops, cabinets, a sink, and a tiny island sat in the middle of the room. It wasn't big by any means, just enough space for three people to move around in.

"You can count on us," I promised.

"Good. Now scram. All of you." He winked at Aunt Aggie. "Get out of my kitchen."

We all hurried back into the dining room. While I had no doubt his bark was worse than his bite, I didn't want to stick around and find out.

"He winked at you, Aunt Aggie!" I giggled and snatched up another cookie.

"He did not!" Aunt Aggie chided.

But I could tell she was pleased.

CHAPTER 3

By seven, Aunt Aggie's open house party was packed with townspeople. Everyone from the mayor to business owners, to every-day citizens were milling around the rooms and hallways eating, drinking, laughing, and having a great time.

"Look who just walked through the door," Peyton said, pointing to the foyer.

I gasped. "It's Temperance Clairmont. She really did come."

Temperance pushed aside a group of five people without bothering to apologize. She was dressed in a black sheath dress with the tiniest threads of silver glitter running throughout, and her white-blonde hair was piled high atop her head. I would place her in her fifties, and even though she was of average height, there was something about her that made her seem taller. I think it was the way she could look up at someone and still manage to somehow look down her nose at the same time.

She stood in the middle of the foyer, eyes narrowed, and carefully surveyed the room. When one side of her nose curled up in disgust, my fists clenched at my sides. If she didn't want to be here, why did she come?

"That's her son Percy."

Startled, I glanced to my left. Mariah stood next to me, tray in hand, eyes brimming with tears.

Percy was dressed in a black pin-striped suit with a dancing Santa tie. His dark eyes matched his dark slicked-back hair and pencil-thin beard. He was trim and nice looking.

"And the flashy woman with him," Mariah said bitterly, "is his *new* fiancée."

"That didn't take long," Raven said.

Mariah shot her a quizzical look. "You know about our breakup?"

I grimaced. "Chef Granger may have mentioned it. Just because he didn't want Aunt Aggie thinking you weren't competent. And the more I talk the worse I'm making things. I'm sorry."

"It's okay," Mariah said. "And, yeah, it didn't take long for him to replace me."

I turned and stared at Temperance, her son, and his fiancée. They looked totally out of their element.

"What's his fiancée's deal?" I asked.

"I'm not sure," Mariah said. "I think I heard she's the back-up weather girl on a local news station."

"Back-up weather girl?" Raven snickered. "Is that even a thing?"

Mariah shrugged. "I guess so."

"And he's already asked her to marry him?" I asked in disbelief. "That's weird."

Percy chose that moment to look our way. When his eyes landed on Mariah, his demeanor instantly changed. His eyes widened and his features softened. He took a small step forward, causing his fiancée to give him the side eye. When she saw where he was looking, her eyes narrowed and she purposely brushed up against Percy and laid her head on his shoulder. It was enough to break the contact between him and Mariah.

"He's obviously not over you," Peyton said.

A tear slid down Mariah's cheek, and she quickly dashed it away.

"Doesn't matter. I'd never marry him as long as his mother is alive. And I pretty much told him that." Mariah laughed sardonically. "Of course, that was right after she told me no uneducated *waitress* would be marrying her son."

"I do like the fiancée's dress though," Peyton said. "Very glamorous."

Raven snorted. "A little much for an open house party."

I studied the red, body-hugging, long dress that was beaded with rhinestones and glitter. Both girls were right...it was a little over-the-top for Copper Cove, but it sure was beautiful. Her strawberry-blonde hair cascaded in loose curls down her back, and her makeup was flawless. She looked like a beauty pageant Miss Claus.

"You're in luck, Mariah," Raven said. "It doesn't look like she's a fan of Temperance, either. Look at the way she's glaring at her."

I chuckled. "Almost like she's wishing the chandelier would fall on her."

"Well that would make two of us," Mariah said.

I laughed.

"I should circulate and hand out these snacks," Mariah said. "But not over there. I can't do that yet."

She turned and circulated throughout the great room, pausing here and there to let people take the goodies off the tray.

"There's my family," Peyton said. "Let's go say hi."

We spent some time laughing and joking with Peyton's parents—and snagging hors d'oeuvres from the passing trays—before heading to the dining room to see if the cookies needed replenishing. And to fuel up on more sugar and caffeine.

"You girls look like you're having fun," Grams said as Henley handed her a coffee.

"We are," I said. "It's fun people watching."

"I saw Lenora," Grams said. "I'm glad she made it out."

Lenora Sanders owned the only movie theater in town. And I'm being generous by calling it a movie theater. It had one room and showed the same movie for a solid month. And it wasn't even a new release movie. Mostly they were old movies...sometimes so old they didn't have color! She and Grams have been friends since childhood.

"I can't believe this turnout," Aunt Aggie gushed as she hurried into the room, careful not to spill her glass of champagne. "I bet there are already fifty people here and we officially *just* opened the doors not even a half hour ago."

Chef Granger strolled out of the kitchen, a huge smile on his face. "I better go mingle real quick before it gets too hectic. Make sure everyone is enjoying the food."

Aunt Aggie set her glass down on the table. "Let me introduce you around."

Chef Granger offered Aunt Aggie his arm, and I smirked at Peyton.

"Here less than a month," Grams grumbled, "and already the men are sniffing around."

"Grams!" I exclaimed. "Shame on you."

Grams shrugged. "What? She always was a bit of a hussy."

"Winnifred," Henley admonished. "Your sister has always been a vibrant, energetic woman."

Grams rolled her eyes. "Like I said...a hussy."

Raven crooked her finger at me. "Let's go see what's hiding in the butler's pantry."

"I suppose we should go make the rounds too," Grams said.

I followed Peyton and Raven into the kitchen. Trays holding tons of tiny, fancy foods lined the countertops. I was about to snag one when Peyton dragged me into the butler's pantry.

"Better goodies to choose from in here," she said.

"Plus we can hide out," Raven said.

We gathered up a handful of cookies and plopped down onto the floor.

"Did you guys notice the way Aunt Aggie and Chef Granger have been acting?" I asked.

Peyton took a huge bite of a sugar cookie and nodded. "Totally. I'm thinking there might be a hookup in their future."

I winced. "Please. It's weird enough I have to think of my *Grams* dating...I don't want to have to go there with Aunt Aggie. It's too much."

Raven gleefully snapped off a gingerbread man's leg.

"You shouldn't look so happy when you do that," I said.

She grinned, shoved the leg in her mouth, then stared me down as she gleefully snapped off the other leg. "I think it's cool the old ladies still have it."

I shuddered. "Just stop."

We ate in silence for a little while longer.

"I don't feel too well," I groaned, holding my stomach.

"Me either," Raven said.

"We just ate six sugar cookies and a handful of gingerbread men," Peyton said. "Of course we aren't going to feel well."

I grinned. "But totally worth it."

We staggered to our feet, laughing and groaning. I was about to open the door when I heard raised voices in the kitchen. I put my finger to my lips and silently slid the door open a few inches.

"Are you threatening me, Temperance?" Chef Granger hissed.

"Just stating a fact," she said. "Now, are you going to fire that girl or not?"

"No."

"I can make you regret that decision," she said.

"I pay my loan to the bank on time every month. You have no hold over me."

"I used to. We were good together once," Temperance purred. "We can be again."

Chef Granger snorted. "We dated for less than a month last year. That's all it took before I saw your true colors."

"Meaning?"

"You're a cruel woman who likes being cruel to others," Chef Granger said. "Look what you did to your son and Mariah."

"You better watch yourself, James," Temperance said. "You forget I sit on the board of directors for the bank."

"Don't threaten me, Temperance," Chef Granger said. "You won't like the outcome."

Temperance laughed. "Is that so? Then I think I *will* call a special bank board meeting Monday. Be prepared to lose your restaurant."

I jerked back when Temperance stalked past the door, simultaneously holding my breath. I had no idea what to do.

"This is *huge*," Peyton whispered.

"I know," I whispered back. "But what do I do now? Do I open the door and risk Chef Granger seeing us?"

Raven reached over, slid the door open, and pushed me out into the kitchen.

And into Chef Granger's path.

CHAPTER 4

"What're you girls doing in here?" Chef Granger asked. "Stealing cookies?"

I cleared my throat. "Guilty as charged."

He looked over my head toward the dining room and frowned. Afraid he'd ask me something I didn't want to admit to—that we'd overheard the argument—I decided to tuck tail and run.

"Well, we better go see how the party is coming along." I turned and pushed against Peyton and Raven. "See ya."

We fled out of the kitchen, through the dining room, and into the great room. I had to find Aunt Aggie and tell her what we'd overheard. Figuring she'd either be in the great room or the formal front parlor, I pushed ahead of the girls and quickly wove through the crowd. When I didn't see her in the great room, I was about to cross the foyer to the parlor when Peyton grabbed hold of my arm.

"Look over there in the corner," she said.

In between the fireplace and the Christmas tree, Temperance and Percy's fiancée stood glaring and hissing at each other, while Percy looked miserable. I tilted my head, letting Peyton and Raven know I wanted to eavesdrop. We stood on the other side of the Christmas tree, pretending to look at the ornaments.

"That's enough." Temperance snatched a glass of champagne out of Percy's hand and plunked it down on the nearest table. "Lay off the booze, Percy."

"Don't you tell my man what to do," Percy's fiancée huffed. "He's not your little boy anymore. He's a *man*."

Temperance raked her eyes over the young woman and scowled. "Best you learn this now, *Barbie*. Percy will always be my son first and foremost. Even if he goes against my wishes and marries you...I will still be in charge. After all, I hold the purse strings."

"As if you'd ever let us forget that," Barbie hissed.

"Not another drink, Percy," Temperance said.

"Yes, mother."

Temperance narrowed her eyes at Barbie before striding across the foyer to the other side of the house.

"It's always 'yes, mother' with you, Percy," Barbie pouted. "When are you going to stand up to her?" She put her hand out and admired the huge engagement ring adorning her hand. It sparkled almost as much as the rhinestones on her dress. "It's *so* unfair she's making me sign a prenup."

Percy nodded, but his eyes were on the glass of champagne his mother had set on the table.

Barbie grinned. "You trust me, don't you, Percy?" She reached over and picked up the glass of champagne and handed it to him. "You know I'm not marrying you for your money, right? You won't make me sign the prenup, will you? You'll stand up to Momma Temperance?"

Percy tossed back the drink in one big gulp. "Sure, babe. Whatever you say."

Peyton tugged at my sleeve, and I turned and followed her and Raven into the foyer. We stopped next to the stairs.

"That's one messed up family," Raven said.

I snickered. "Aren't we all?"

Raven shook her head. "Not like that."

24

"I want to find Aunt Aggie," I said, "and tell her about Chef Granger and Temperance having words."

"Do you think Aggie's in the parlor or the library?" Peyton asked.

I snatched an hors d'oeuvre off a passing tray and popped it into my mouth. "Let's try the front parlor."

"The front parlor is packed," a young male voice said behind me.

Turning, I frowned at the guy standing there. I knew I should know his name, but he was a year under me in school.

"Brandon Powell," he said.

"Junior, right?" Peyton asked.

He nodded at her, his ears turning pink. Not that it should be a surprise, a lot of guys went pink when they looked at Peyton.

"You here with your mom and dad?" I asked.

Brandon winced and shuffled his feet. "Not exactly."

"Then what exactly?" Raven asked.

Brandon cleared his throat and looked around the foyer. No one paid us any attention, but I guess he wanted to make sure.

"Um, my dad is here looking for Temperance Clairmont," he mumbled. "Do you know her?"

I scoffed. "Not very well. But from what I've seen of her tonight, she's pretty good at throwing shade."

Brandon, Peyton, and Raven laughed.

"We've been dealing with her for about three years now," Brandon said. "We rent from her."

Peyton patted his arm. "I'm sorry. She seems like a difficult woman to deal with."

Brandon looked down at her hand and blushed again. "That's why my dad's looking for her. We went out to her big fancy house and the butler guy told us she wasn't home. When Dad lost his temper and threatened the poor guy, he finally told us Mrs. Clairmont was in town at some party."

"Which led you here," Raven said. "Your dad looking for trouble, Brandon?"

I hid my smile. Leave it to a girl whose parents are both lawyers to ask the tough questions.

"I hope not," he whispered. "I really do. We can't afford any more trouble."

"What's going on?" I asked.

Brandon blew out a breath. "We got an eviction notice today."

"Oh Brandon," Peyton said. "I'm so sorry."

Again Brandon didn't say anything, just looked all moony-eyed at Peyton. It was all I could do not to roll my eyes. Peyton honestly had no idea the guy was going all puppy love when he looked at her.

"What did Temperance say in the eviction notice?" I asked.

"She said we have to pay the back rent immediately or we're out in three days. We were almost caught up, so I don't know why she's suddenly done this."

I bit my lip. I wanted to ask how they'd gotten behind, but I didn't want to seem insensitive.

"How'd you guys get behind?" Raven asked.

"It's just me, my dad, and my little sister, ya know? My mom ran out about four years ago when Jillian was just a baby. Dad's a commercial fisherman. A little over a month

26

ago, he sliced his hand and arm deep enough he did some nerve damage and had to have like a hundred stitches. It laid him up a couple weeks. He's still not fully recovered, but at least he's back to work. I tried to help him after school, but it wasn't enough to keep up with our bills. We fell a little behind, but we're almost caught up now."

Raven clucked her tongue. "And now Temperance is threatening to kick you out the week of Christmas? Not cool."

"I'm trying to find a part-time job," Brandon said. "Something I can do after school and on the weekends, just to help out. But I'm not having much luck. Not many people want to hire a kid."

I gasped. "I may know of something. Do you have your license?"

"Yeah. But I don't have a car."

"You may not need one," I said. "Just a license. Let me talk some more to the people looking, and I'll get back with you."

Brandon's face lit up. "That would be gre—"

"Unhand me, you vulgar man!"

Temperance's shrill voice rang out from the front parlor. The conversation in the foyer stopped and everyone turned toward the commotion. Not wanting to miss anything, I linked hands with Peyton and Raven and pushed aside the people standing around.

Inside the parlor, a thin, middle-aged man with a full-sized beard, sunken eyes, hollowed cheeks, and scraggly clothes reached out and grabbed hold of a shocked Temperance.

"Did you not hear me?" she screeched. "I said unhand me this instant."

"Please. I just need to speak with you," the man said.

"Dad!" Brandon pushed past us and ran to his dad's side.

"It's okay, Brandon." His dad waved a piece of paper in the air. "I just want to speak with her about this."

Temperance shook off the grip on her arm and looked down her nose at the disheveled man. "I assumed you could read, Mr. Powell. My apologies." Temperance patted her helmet hair into place. "It says if you don't pay me your back rent immediately, you will be kicked out in three days." She narrowed her eyes. "Is that simple enough?"

Mr. Powell's face went red, but I didn't know if it was from anger or embarrassment. I looked at Brandon, and my heart lurched. Poor guy looked like he wanted to cry...or have the floor swallow him whole. I understood that feeling. I had it a lot.

"Please, Mrs. Clairmont," Mr. Powell said. "I really just need—"

"You really just need to pay me my money," Temperance snapped before turning and sweeping out of the room.

Merriment & Murder

Chapter 5

I hurried into the parlor, Peyton and Raven on my heels. I could hear people murmuring and pointing, but I ignored them.

"Are you okay?" I asked Brandon's dad.

Mr. Powell blinked a couple times then shook his head. "No, young lady. I'm *not* okay." He looked at his son and smiled sadly. "But I guess this isn't the first time we've struggled. Is it, son?"

"No, Dad, it's not." Brandon rested his hand on his dad's arm. "Let's just go home. We'll think of something."

Mr. Powell's eyes narrowed as he gazed out of the room where Temperance had just exited. "You stay here with your friends, Brandon. I need to see to a few more things."

Mr. Powell gave Brandon a quick smile before stalking out of the parlor. I caught the eyes of Mayor Barrow and his wife by the picture window. They weren't exactly fans of mine...seeing as how I'd publicly accused the mayor of killing Prudence Livingston last month.

"You okay?" Peyton asked Brandon.

He nodded. "Yeah. Dad'll be fine. Listen, I think I saw a huge table filled with cookies. I want to go snag some and bring them back for Jillian. She's staying the night across the street with one of her friends tonight. But I know she'd love a handful of these cookies. Thanks for everything."

"If I hear anything more about the job," I said, "I'll let you know."

"Thanks, Brynn. That's real nice of you."

Peyton sighed and wrapped her arms around me as Brandon shuffled out of the parlor. "I feel sorry for him."

"Me too," Raven said. "I mean, I don't know him or anything, but it's gotta be hard to only have one parent and barely making ends meet."

I knew all too well the feeling of having no parent want me. Thankfully Grams gave me all the love I needed. And we'd never had to struggle financially. Not like Brandon and his dad.

"Remind me when the party is over," I said, "to tell Grams how much I appreciate all she's done for me. And though I'd never admit it to her, I'm glad she's had the apothecary all these years."

Peyton laughed. "Your secret is safe with us."

"C'mon," Raven said. "I need some sugar."

I decided to cut through the back way of the house in hopes of finding Aunt Aggie. We took a left out of the parlor and shuffled past the people standing in the wide hallway. I peeked in at the library to see if Aunt Aggie was in there, but there were only a handful of people browsing the books. At the end of the corridor we could either go right or left. Left leading to the bathroom and Aunt Aggie's private quarters, and right leading to the kitchen entrance opposite the dining room.

I took a right and walked into the kitchen.

"Well, this looks like trouble heading my way," Chef Granger joked when he saw us.

Aunt Aggie walked out of the butler's pantry holding a tray of cookies. "There you girls are. I've been looking for you."

My eyes darted between Chef Granger and her. "I've been looking for you too."

"What's up?" she asked.

I looked at Chef Granger again. He gave me a quick smile before adding more hors d'oeuvres to a tray.

"Oh, nothing much," I said. "I can tell you later."

"Well, then here." She thrust the tray of cookies at me. "Go replenish the cookies out there. I can see two trays almost empty from here."

Chef Granger glanced at his watch. "We still have a little over an hour for the party. How are cookie supplies in the butler's pantry looking?"

"No need to worry," Aunt Aggie said, giving me a piercing look. "As long as little nibblers stay out of supplies, we'll have enough to last the rest of the party."

I gave her a grin before grabbing the tray from her.

"Everyone looks to be having a wonderful time," Peyton said.

Aunt Aggie nodded. "I think so too."

Peyton continued to talk with Aunt Aggie, but my attention was focused elsewhere. Out of the corner of my eye, near the far end of the dining room, Thomas Baskins and his wife, Beatrice, were in a heated exchange. I couldn't make out what they were saying from here, but it was intense, whatever it was.

Thomas owned the diner in town off Pacific Drive. He'd recently married Beatrice, one of his waitresses, two years ago. About once every four months, Grams and I ate breakfast there on a Saturday morning before we opened the apothecary.

"I'll just go put these down," I said.

I hurried into the dining room. Averting my gaze, I placed the tray in the middle of the long table, then carefully arranged the cookies so all the trays looked full...still keeping an ear on the fighting couple.

I wasn't sure why I was so enthralled with all the drama going on around me. Usually I avoided drama like the plague, but lately I couldn't help it. Especially after solving the murders last month. It was like I was addicted to figuring things out.

"But I *saw* you staring at her," Beatrice hissed.

"You saw nothing," Thomas growled back. "It's just your imagination. Now stop making a spectacle of yourself, Beatrice."

Beatrice's lower lip trembled, and she glanced around the room. I averted my gaze and continued shuffling the cookies so she wouldn't see I'd overheard everything.

"You're just jealous that I used to date her," Thomas said.

Beatrice stood taller. "I wouldn't have to be jealous if you'd stop chasing after her."

Thomas snorted. "Chasing? Really? Just stop."

"Me?" Beatrice's voice rose, and I couldn't help but look over at them.

And I wasn't the only one watching. The man getting coffee at the buffet paused to listen in, as did about four other couples gathering up cookies.

Thomas grabbed Beatrice's arm, but she shook it off. "You're the one who needs to remember Temperance dumped you over three years ago. Remember?"

"I remember," Thomas gritted out.

"She's a horrible, shallow woman, and yet you still have feelings for her while being married to me."

I held my breath, waiting to see what Thomas would say or do next. It was shocking to hear them speak about something so intimate. I saw them around town and visited their diner. I just figured they were happily married because they were together.

Thomas leaned in, and I caught myself doing the same.

"Watch what you say next, Beatrice," Thomas whispered, "or I'm going to assume you're ready to call it quits. And lay off the champagne, you know what it does to you."

I jerked back upright when he turned and stalked past the table, shoving guests aside. Beatrice's body and shoulders shook, but she turned toward the wall to hide her face.

"What's going on?" Raven hissed in my ear. "That Thomas guy from the diner looks mad enough to kill."

"I'll tell you guys later," I whispered back. "Right now, let's go cheer up Beatrice."

The three of us headed to the corner where Beatrice was trying to hold it all together. When I placed my hand on her shoulder, she let out a little sob.

"Hey Beatrice," I said perkily. "I really like your outfit."

Beatrice sniffed then looked down at herself.

"Thanks, Brynn. That's nice of you to say so."

Truth was, it was kind of hideous. It was one of those Christmas sweaters that you couldn't always tell if it was supposed to be dressy or tacky. It was cream colored with three large Christmas trees on the front. The bulbs were glittery and bright. But since she'd paired it with a black skirt, I figured it was supposed to be dressy and not tacky.

"I love the way it shimmers in the light," Beatrice said, running her hands lightly down the front of her body.

I stepped back when little flakes of glitter fell to the floor.

Beatrice drained the last of her champagne and looked around for a place to set the glass. I could tell she was a little unsteady on her feet.

"Let me take that for you," Peyton said. "Do you need another?"

No. I think she's had plenty.

"No thanks," Beatrice said softly. "But it's nice of you girls to ask."

"You doing okay?" I asked.

Beatrice wiped at a tear that slid down her cheek. "No. Not really. I've always known deep down things weren't what they should be, but I let it go."

I ignored Peyton's quizzical look, and when Raven opened her mouth to say something, I shook my head. I didn't want them interrupting Beatrice's words.

"I mean, when we first got together, I knew he was rebounding from Temperance. But I fell for Thomas the day he hired me to work at the diner five years ago. I thought I could make him love me when he finally agreed to date. I could tell he still loved Temperance, but I thought I could change him." She snorted. "And then I stupidly married him."

"I'm so sorry," I said.

34

I knew my eyes had to be as wide as pancakes. Usually people still saw me as a kid and didn't divulge juicy stuff like this to me.

"And then when that fancy chef guy came to town last year to open his restaurant, and he started seeing Temperance, I thought everything would be better. Ya know?" Beatrice sighed. "But they didn't stay together long, and my hopes were dashed."

"Do you mean Chef Granger?" I asked.

Beatrice nodded. "Yes. He and Temperance started seeing each other, and I couldn't have been happier. But it didn't last long, and I was once again forced to face the fact that my new husband wasn't in love with me like he should be."

"That's awful," Peyton said. "I'm really sorry, Beatrice."

Beatrice shrugged and stepped out of our circle. "Maybe Santa will grant my wish this year and permanently remove Temperance from my life. Now, if you'll excuse me girls, I really need to use the restroom and fix my face."

CHAPTER 6

"That's a really sad story," Peyton said. "I'm seriously depressed now."

Raven reached over and grabbed a snowman sugar cookie, then shoved it at Peyton. "Here, eat this. It'll make you happy again."

Looking around the nearly empty room, I realized it must be getting late because the crowd seemed to be thinning out.

"Let's go find Grams and Henley," I said.

"Or my parents," Raven said. "I haven't seen them around yet."

"Let's cut back through the kitchen and head to the library," I suggested.

I was surprised to see Chef Granger wasn't in the kitchen when we hurried through, but I did happen to catch a glimpse of Beatrice standing in line waiting for the restroom down the hallway that led to Aunt Aggie's personal area.

I slipped into the library and looked around. The chandelier lights were set on dim and the flicker of candles in the sconces around the room gave off an ominous vibe. This was my favorite room in the B&B. The front of the library held four comfy chairs guests could sit in and read. The bookshelves lined the back of the room, and to give the room a more private feel, Aunt Aggie had installed another bookshelf in the center of the room to break up the large area. Next to the center bookshelf sat one of those old-fashioned chairs that were tall and ornate. I think it was called a Victorian chair or something. It had brown arms and legs with pink velvet fabric...and was ugly as sin.

I waved at Raven's parents standing by the French doors that led outside. They were pretty cool as far as parents went. Her mom was kind of hard-nosed and stern, but her dad was a total riot. Every time I saw him he had a funny joke to tell me.

"Look at you girls," Mrs. Masters said. "You look beautiful."

"Sure do," Mr. Masters agreed. "Hey, I got one for ya."

Raven groaned. "Dad!"

"Why are Christmas trees so bad at knitting?" he asked.

We all looked at each other and shrugged.

"They always drop their needles!" he cried.

We all laughed at his delivery, which was almost as funny as the joke itself.

"I got one for you," I said.

Mr. Masters raised an eyebrow. "Let's hear it."

I grinned. "What do you call Santa's helpers?"

He lifted a finger to his lips in thought. After a few seconds he sighed. "I give up. What do you call Santa's helpers?"

"Subordinate clauses," I declared proudly.

"That's a good one!" Mr. Masters laughed and wrapped me in a one-arm hug, and it was all I could do not to wrap my arms around him and hug him back.

Even though I was getting used to his easy display of affection, it still sometimes took me by surprise. I'd never had a dad, so I wasn't used to having a man hug me. Raven usually just rolled her eyes and laughed along with her dad...and I tried to do the same. But deep down, I didn't want to roll my eyes at him...because deep down there was a part of me that was jealous of Raven. And of Peyton. They both had dads that hugged them, told silly jokes, and did normal things like that with them.

"What're you girls up to?" Mr. Masters asked.

"Just making sure everyone's having fun," I said.

"I think the party is winding down," Mrs. Masters said. "Your dad and I were just talking about leaving, Raven."

"Okay," Raven said. "I'm going to stay the night with Brynn and Peyton."

While Raven talked with her parents, I walked over to the chair to peek around the corner to see if anyone else was in the library. I rested my arms on the back of the ugly Victorian chair and tried not to act surprised when I saw Temperance Clairmont and Thomas Baskins deep in conversation toward the back of the room.

When he placed a hand on her arm, she flung it off and said something to him. Whatever it was, it made his face turn red and his eyes narrow. But she didn't seem to care, because she'd turned and was headed right for me!

Gasping, I turned and hurried back over to where Peyton and Raven stood with Mr. and Mrs. Masters. I pretended not to notice when Temperance swept past us and out of the room. Taking a peek over my shoulder, my eyes nearly fell out of my head when I noticed Thomas staring at me. A few seconds later he strode out the door, leaving us alone in the library.

"You girls have fun tonight," Mrs. Masters said. "Don't stay up too late."

Raven rolled her eyes and gave them a hug before we all walked out of the library. Since the library was now empty, I decided to shut the door.

"Party is definitely winding down," Mr. Masters said. "Just fifteen minutes ago I could hardly walk down the corridor without bumping into someone."

We waved goodbye to them in the foyer. I looked around to see if I spotted Jessica or Janice, but I didn't see them anywhere. They must have slipped out earlier.

"There's Aunt Aggie, Grams, and Henley," I said, pointing inside the front parlor. "And they're talking with Temperance, Percy, and Barbie. Let's go!"

We hurried inside the parlor. I counted only about ten people inside the room, which made it easier to get around. I sidled up next to Barbie as Peyton and Raven stood over by Temperance.

"I was just telling Temperance here," Aunt Aggie said, "that I found a book on the origins of Copper Cove in the library."

"Really?" I perked up at that. I knew my Grams' family had been founding members over two hundred years ago, but I didn't really know anything else about the other founding families.

"Your aunt offered to let me borrow it," Temperance said, somehow making it sound like it was beneath her. "I'm eager to look it over. I'm sure my family will be mentioned in there. Your family wasn't the only founding member of this great town."

Aunt Aggie gave me a grin, and I could tell she was thinking what I was thinking...big whoop-de-doo.

"I'll go grab it for you if you'd like," Aunt Aggie said.

Temperance held up her hand. "I can find it on my own. You said in the back of the room, second bookshelf over?"

Aunt Aggie nodded. "Yes. Feel free to take it and keep it as long as you need."

"Thank you," Temperance said. "I think after I grab the book, we'll be heading out." She glanced over at Percy and Barbie. "I believe we'd had enough fun as a family for one evening."

Barbie slid her arm through Percy's. "Quite so Momma Temperance. Percy and I are ready whenever you are."

Temperance nodded once. "Percy, I'll meet you both in the foyer in five minutes."

Raven gave me a sly smile as the older lady walked stiffly out of the room. Obviously I wasn't the only one that thought she was a piece of work.

My mouth dropped when I saw Temperance grab Mariah's arm and forcibly push her to the side of the stairs, away from prying eyes.

"I think I left my drink in the great room," I said. "I'll be right back."

I shot out of the circle before anyone could stop me. Slipping from the room, I kept my back to the side of the stairs and got as close as I could to the two fighting women.

"I may not like her, but she's a better substitute than you," Temperance said. "And once she signs the prenup, it won't matter. All that matters is that Percy doesn't end up with a loser like you."

"You're a horrible beast of a woman," Mariah said. "I hope to make you choke on those words one day."

40

Having heard enough, I walked quickly back into the parlor and joined everyone again.

"Where's your drink?" Aunt Aggie asked.

"Oh," I said, "it wasn't in there."

Peyton and Raven gave me quizzical looks, but I ignored them.

"Ya know," Barbie said, "I better go see if Momma Temperance needs any help finding that book."

Turning quickly, Barbie sashayed out of the room so fast her rhinestones were practically popping off her skin-tight dress.

"Can I get you girls to do me a favor?" Aunt Aggie asked when Percy grabbed a flute of champagne and excused himself.

"Sure," I said.

"Go out back and bring in some more wood, please. The fireplace could use a couple more logs."

"You bet," I said.

We headed down the hallway, past the closed library, and around the corner into the kitchen. Chef Granger had his hand on Mariah's shoulder, and she was wiping away tears. I knew it was about what I'd just overheard by the stairs, so we continued silently by, not disturbing them.

I opened the sliding glass door in the dining room that led to the conservatory. Aunt Aggie had decorated it mostly in white, with greenery from the live plants as the only pop of color.

Opening another glass-paneled door that led outside, I turned back to Peyton and Raven. "I'm exhausted. I can't wait for everyone to leave so we can get out of these clothes and go to bed."

"I hear you," Raven said. "These shoes are killing me."

Peyton tossed back her glossy mane of blonde hair and laughed. "I disagree. I love wearing dress-up clothes."

I rolled my eyes and reached down to grab a piece of wood off the stack when I heard voices around the corner. Putting my finger to my lips, I motioned the girls to follow me.

Peeking around the corner, Temperance and Barbie were nose-to-nose in the side yard, and the door to the library was wide open. I squinted even harder and realized Peyton's little brother, Brady, was hiding behind a tree not five feet away.

CHAPTER 7

I was so focused on Brady that I missed what was said, but Temperance slammed back inside the library and Barbie whirled around and threw her glass of champagne across the yard. Thankfully she missed the tree Brady was hiding behind, and the glass landed with a soft thud in the grass.

I motioned the girls to follow me, and I sprinted across the yard to where Brady was still crouched down behind the tree. It was then I noticed Jinx was with him.

Meow!

"I just wanted to come outside and pet the kitty." His voice was high and his eyes were huge.

As if on cue, we dropped our wood and crouched down beside him.

"It's okay, Brady," Peyton said. "It's over."

For the first time that night, I realized I hadn't seen Jinx inside much. Reaching down, I ran my hand across Jinx's back as I stared at Brady.

"You okay?" I asked.

Brady nodded, but I could hear his shaky breath coming in small pants from his skinny little body.

"Remember how we paid you a buck last month to spy for us?" I asked.

Brady looked up and grinned. "Yeah. And I remember I said I wouldn't do it for a buck next time you needed me."

I pretended to think that over, but really I was just letting him get his courage back. "Did you overhear what they were saying?"

"Yeah. And if you want to know what was said, it'll cost you five bucks. I don't work for free no more ladies."

"Five bucks?" I exclaimed. "I'm not sure it's worth five dollars to know what was said."

Brady stood up and looked around the empty yard. We followed his lead and stood up as well.

"I can't tell you all of it," Brady said honestly. "Mom would make me lick the soap bar if I did."

I laughed. "Did one of them say a bad word?"

"Yeah. The one with the pretty sparkly dress. She said a word so bad I bet Mom wouldn't just make her lick the soap bar, she'd make her *eat* the whole thing."

We all laughed at that...including Jinx.

"I don't have the cash on me right now," I said, "but I'll get it to you. What happened?"

"The pretty lady in the sparkly dress said over her dead body would she sign the preshall."

I frowned. "The preshall?"

Brady nodded solemnly as Jinx meowed and jumped up into his arms. "Yep. The preshall agreement."

"You mean prenuptial agreement?" Raven asked.

Brady shrugged. "Guess so. It was something like that. Then the older lady told the sparkly one if she didn't sign it, then she'd never marry her son, and the sparkly lady called her a really, really, *reeealllly* bad name. The older lady just laughed at it, though. Which was weird. Then the older lady walked back inside the house there, and the sparkly lady threw her glass at me." His eyes got big again, and he hugged Jinx closer. "I thought she knew I was there and was going to hurt me."

44

Peyton wrapped her arms around her little brother. "No one's gonna hurt you, Brady. Promise."

"That's all I know," Brady said. "But I'm kinda disappointed you didn't need to lift me up and look through windows like you did last time."

I laughed. "The night is still young, kid. You never know."

He grinned. "Yeah. You never know." He set Jinx down on the ground. "Mom and Dad are ready to go. I only came out here to say goodbye to Jinx. I guess I better get back inside so we can leave."

He waved and raced back to the front of the house.

"That Temperance is one mean lady," Peyton said. "I'm about ready to give her and that Barbie girl a piece of my mind for scaring Brady like that."

"I don't know about you guys," I said, "but I've seen nothing but fighting and ugliness tonight. Not at all what Christmas is supposed to be about."

Raven snorted. "I remember one Christmas where I had to hang out at a police station with my dad because he'd been hired to represent an adult man who'd gotten into a fight with his brother over who received the best present."

Peyton and I laughed, but I was also sort of horrified.

"That's no lie," Raven said. "So this drama isn't anything."

I reached down and picked up my piece of wood. "Let's get this inside before Aunt Aggie sends out a search party for us."

"Hey there!"

Brandon waved at us from the front lawn.

We waved back and headed toward him.

"Dad and I are heading out soon," he said. "It was a great party."

I was about to tell him to have a good vacation, when his dad rushed outside and grabbed Brandon by the sleeve.

"We need to leave," his dad said. "Now."

Brandon sent his dad a quizzical look. "Okay."

"Now."

Without another word, the two men hurried down the sidewalk and into the night.

"That was odd," I said.

"Parents are odd," Raven said.

I snorted. "I'll take your word for it."

We walked up the porch steps and headed toward the great room. It took a few extra minutes since six or seven guests chose that time to leave. After wishing them a Merry Christmas and answering all their questions about school and plans for vacation, we were finally on the move again.

I followed Peyton and Raven into the great room and dumped the wood next to the fireplace. Brushing the wood chips off my dress, I barely gave Percy a nod as he exited the dining room and sidled up to us.

"I decided to grab a cookie before heading out," he said. "I suppose I should go find Mother and Barbie."

"Last time we saw them," Peyton said, "both Temperance and Barbie were in the library."

More like in the side yard having an argument, but close enough.

"Did I hear my name mentioned?" Barbie cooed as she wrapped her arms through Percy's.

46

"There you are," Percy said. "Where's Mother?"

"I don't know honey," Barbie said. "The door to the library was closed when I went to help Momma Temperance get the book. So I just went on ahead and used the little girls' room."

Liar!

"We'll go look for her," I told Percy. "Maybe she started reading the book and lost track of time."

I jerked my head to Peyton and Raven for them to follow me. Aunt Aggie was standing by the front door thanking people for stopping by. There were probably less than twenty people left milling around in the house.

"Did you hear Barbie lie?" I asked as we headed to the library.

"Sure did," Raven said. "But then again, what's she gonna say?"

I stopped in front of the closed door. "She's right. The door *is* still closed."

Turning the knob, I pushed the door open and we stepped inside.

Meow!

Jinx shot into the library and immediately spotted something on the floor. He patted it with his paw a couple times.

Peyton bent down and gasped. "Look what it is."

She handed me a rhinestone. I couldn't be sure, but I'd bet anything it was from Barbie's dress. Granted, there were a lot of sparkles and glitter tonight, but something in my gut told me it belonged to Barbie.

"Mrs. Clairmont?" I called out as I slipped the rhinestone into the pocket of my dress. "Are you in here?"

Silence.

"Maybe she's in the kitchen stalking Chef Granger?" Raven snickered.

"We'll check there next," I said.

We walked toward the center of the room where the bookshelf and Victorian chair sat facing the back of the room.

"Mrs. Clairmont? Are you back here?" I took a step around the chair and screamed.

Chapter 8

"What is it?" Peyton rushed to my side.

I didn't say anything...just pointed.

Temperance Clairmont was slouched in the chair, her head at an odd angle, and her eyes wide open. A red and green scarf was wrapped around her throat.

"Move aside," Peyton demanded. "I need to see before the adults come in."

Peyton not only helped her dad out at the funeral home and went on calls with him as the coroner for the county, but she was also leaning toward becoming a medical examiner once we graduated from high school.

"Hurry," Raven said. "Brynn's scream is sure to bring them in any second now."

I rolled my eyes. "Well, excuse me for not being in control of my emotions."

"I also just texted my dad," Raven said, "and told him to get back to the party ASAP."

Peyton wrapped the sleeve of her dress around her hand and carefully peeled back the scarf. We all leaned in to see.

"Definite sign of ligature marks," Peyton said. "Dad will have to declare it, but I'd say no doubt she was strangled."

"The scarf still wrapped around her throat helps," I said dryly.

Peyton looked down her nose at me, and I immediately felt contrite. It wasn't her fault I became snarky when I was upset.

"There's some glitter on her hands," Raven noted. "Probably even under her nails, but I can't tell without turning over her hands. And I don't want to do that. But I'd say she put up a fight."

"That pretty much makes everyone a suspect," I said. "Even the men. I saw a couple guys here tonight with glitter on their Christmas ties."

"What's going on in here?" Mayor Barrow thundered from the doorway. "I thought I heard screaming."

"You need to call Chief Baedie," Raven said. "We have a murder."

"What?"

Mayor Barrow started toward us, but Raven held up her hand. "Seriously, Mayor. You need to call 911."

It didn't take but a few more seconds before the library's doorway became jam packed with people vying for a look inside. Mayor Barrow yanked his cell phone out of his pocket and started speaking into it at once.

"Move aside," Aunt Aggie called. "It's my library. I'll see what's going on."

Some of the crowd had moved inside the library, and I tried to memorize who was there and who wasn't. I didn't see Chef Granger or Barbie.

"Chief Baedie should be here in a few minutes," Mayor Barrow said.

"I need to see the body," Mr. Patterson said as he pushed through the crowd. "I was just heading home when I heard someone might need my services."

Peyton's dad gave us a quick nod before kneeling down next to the chair to examine Temperance. He was still looking over the body when Mr. Masters pushed his way into the room. He looked like he'd sprinted all the way from his house when he got Raven's text.

"She's dead," Mr. Patterson said to Mayor Barrow.

"What's going on?" Percy Clairmont asked. "Someone said my mom was in here. Mom?"

Mr. Masters stepped forward and held Percy back when he broke free of the crowd and tried to rush into the library.

"Let go of me!" Percy demanded. "I need to see my mother."

"I'm afraid your mother is dead, Percy," Mr. Patterson said.

"What? No, she's not. She came in here to get a book and then we were going home."

Percy tried to push past Mr. Masters again, but Raven's dad was strong. He was finally able to get Percy to sit in one of the chairs at the front of the library.

I knew I should be memorizing who all was still around, who seemed upset and who didn't, but unfortunately I wasn't as cool as I should be...I mean, seeing as how I seemed to have developed a knack for stumbling over dead bodies.

"Is it true?" Thomas Baskins asked from the doorway.

I tried looking behind him to see where Beatrice was, but he was too tall. I couldn't see over him.

"Okay, okay. Move aside, Thomas. Chief coming through."

I rolled my eyes at Raven when Chief Baedie pushed his bulky body into the library. He paused beside Percy and Mr. Masters and hitched up his sagging pants.

"What's going on here?" he demanded.

"What's going on is Temperance Clairmont is dead," I said.

"And you might want to move everyone back," Peyton added, "because they are contaminating the crime scene the more they push into the library."

Chief Baedie's face flushed before he turned back to the crowd. "Go on. Nothing to see here. Go on home."

Aunt Aggie dropped down into one of the chairs and shook her head. "I can't believe this."

I rushed over to her side. "It'll be okay. We'll figure this out."

"You won't be doing nothing," Chief Baedie said. "You hear me? You leave this to the professionals. I don't need you kids snooping around like you did last month."

"You mean last month when we solved your case for you?" I asked.

Chief Baedie narrowed his eyes. "You didn't—"

"What's going on in here, Brynn?" Grams asked as she pulled Henley through the crowd and stepped inside the library.

Chief Baedie threw up his hands. "Where're my guys? Get these people out of here! Take down their names and send them home. This party is over!"

I tried to scan the crowd once more, but two policemen came into view and started moving everyone along.

"Let me see the body," Chief Baedie demanded.

"Over here, Chief." Mr. Patterson and the chief walked over to Temperance's body while Barbie and Percy stood by silently watching.

"Does anyone know who the scarf belongs to?" Chief Baedie asked.

Aunt Aggie stood up and walked over to the chair. "It's mine. I usually hang it on the hook over there by the doors."

I tried thinking back to whether or not I'd seen the scarf earlier in the evening, and I honestly couldn't remember. I remembered seeing Raven's parents by the door, but I couldn't remember if the scarf was there or not.

Chief Baedie stood up and rocked back on his heels. "Looks like your place is shut down until I solve this case."

"What?" Aunt Aggie exclaimed. "You can't do that! I'm due to have my first guests on Wednesday, Christmas Eve."

Chief Baedie smacked his lips together. "Not my problem. What I got here is the dead body of a prominent woman in this town, your scarf as the murder weapon, and the murder took place in your house." He looked her up and down. "Now that I think about it, you might want to find you a good lawyer."

Aunt Aggie threw up her hands. "Oh, please! Why on earth would I want to kill someone I didn't even really know?"

Chief Baedie shrugged. "Dunno. But I'm sure I'll figure it out. I want you to give me a detailed list of everyone who attended tonight. I'll pick it up in the morning."

Aunt Aggie's mouth dropped open. "I can't do that. I have no idea who all was here tonight. I'm still relatively new in town."

Chief Baedie flicked his eyes over to Grams. "I'm sure Winnie can help you with the list." He turned back to Aunt Aggie. "I mean it. First thing in the morning I'll be here expecting a list." He placed a hand on Percy's shoulder, but his eyes never left Aunt Aggie. "Not to worry, son, I'll find out who killed your momma."

I'd heard enough. "Chief Baedie, I witnessed at least six people tonight have motive to kill Temperance. So you might want to lay off my aunt and focus on the real killer."

"We'll get to that." Chief Baedie narrowed his eyes. "Let me guess, you three girls just *happened* to stumble across the body, right?"

I crossed my arms over my chest. "That's right."

Mr. Masters held up his hand. "Chief, if you are going to question the girls tonight, I'm going to insist you do it with me present."

Chief Baedie sighed. "Then let's get this over with. Who's first?"

CHAPTER 9

By the time Chief Baedie finished questioning Peyton, Raven, and me, it was after ten o'clock, and I was dead tired. The three of us shuffled into the dining room where Grams, Henley, Aunt Aggie, Chef Granger, and Jinx were sitting around the table.

"Where's Mariah and the other servers?" I asked.

"I sent them home," Chef Granger said. "We've all had a tough night."

I couldn't help but wonder how much celebrating Mariah would do tonight now that Temperance was dead. Would she try and get back with Percy, even though he had a fiancée?

Mr. Masters leaned against the door jamb. "The police just finished processing the scene and are ready to leave."

Aunt Aggie stood. "I better go see them out."

I glanced over at Chef Granger. He didn't look upset, but then again, I really didn't know him all that well.

"I'm sorry about Temperance," I said.

He lifted an eyebrow. "Thanks."

"I got the feeling you two knew each other," I said.

One corner of his mouth lifted in a smile. "I guess you could say that."

Knew her very *well if Beatrice is correct.*

"C'mon, Brynn," Raven said. "I'm ready for bed. Let's go across the street to your place. We can talk about this later."

Meow! Meow!

I nodded. "Sure, Jinx. You can come with us. See you guys in the morning."

The four of us hurried across the street and up to my bedroom on the second floor. I quickly changed into my pajamas and sat cross-legged on my bed.

Meow! Meoooow!

I held up my hand. "I know. I know. I got it."

"Whatcha got?" Peyton asked as she sat at the foot of the bed.

"Jinx says we need to step up and solve this case. It's the least we can do for Aunt Aggie."

Raven yawned and plopped down on the other side of the bed. "We saw enough tonight to have definite suspects and motives."

"Yep." I grabbed a notebook from my side table. "All we need are alibis."

"Let's make a list," Peyton said.

We worked for about ten minutes getting down everyone we thought should be a suspect and their motives. It came out to be quite a few people.

"Read it," Raven demanded. "Make sure we got everyone."

I sighed. "Fine. Then we go to bed. I'm exhausted."

Raven motioned for me to read.

"I have Percy, the son. I don't really see him as a big contender, but we did see him have words with his mom, and he's due to inherit big time I'm sure." I put a check by his name. "Next is Barbie. Lots of tension. We saw her practically physically fight with Temperance, she was still at the party, and one of the last people to see Temperance alive. Motive to kill would be she didn't want to sign the prenup and by getting rid of Temperance, she wouldn't have to."

"Plus we have the rhinestone," Peyton said.

I gasped. "Oh man! I forgot I put it in my dress pocket! That's probably key evidence."

"That we tampered with," Peyton said.

"Technically," I said, "Jinx tampered with it."

Meow!

He glared at me from the window seat he was perched in.

"What?" I asked. "You did. Your paw prints were on it first."

"Regardless of who tampered with it first," Raven said, "it now just means we have to prove it belongs to Barbie. It won't go to show beyond a reasonable doubt she killed Temperance, but it *is* evidence."

"You sound more like a prosecuting attorney like your mom instead of a defense attorney like your dad," I joked.

"Yeah," Peyton agreed. "Which way do you think you'll lean toward after law school?"

"I don't know," Raven said. "I still have a long time to decide."

I looked back down at the list. "Okay. Then there's Mariah. We know she was once engaged to Percy, and from the sparks flying off them tonight, they still seem to love each other."

Raven snorted. "Stop romanticizing it. He's a grown man in love with a woman his mom doesn't approve of so he does nothing. He's a coward."

"I have to agree," Peyton says. "Which is why even though we've said he's a suspect, I look at how weak he is emotionally, and can't really see him as the killer."

"But Mariah could be," I said. "Not only were sparks flying between Percy and Mariah...but they were also flying between Temperance and Mariah, just not in a gooey love way. That was pure hate I overheard by the staircase."

"I remember seeing Mariah in the kitchen with Chef Granger just before going outside to get wood," Raven said. "It could be after she left the kitchen she went down the side hallway that leads to the library, saw Temperance go in, then Barbie. Maybe she heard the fight, and then when Barbie came in the front door, she went inside the library to confront Temperance. They had another fight and then Mariah strangled her."

"Wow," I said, "that's pretty good."

Raven gave me a small smile. "Practicing."

Peyton pointed at me. "And Mariah did say she wouldn't marry Percy as long as his mother was still alive."

"True," I agreed. "Then we have Chef Granger."

"Not as strong a suspect," Raven said.

I snorted. "You don't want him guilty because then you'd lose your weekly meal out."

Raven grinned. "You're probably right."

"He and Temperance had a fight in the kitchen," I said, "and she threatened to call a board meeting at the bank to call in his note. Plus there's the implication of a brief affair. He was still at the party, and we know of at least two or three times we went into the kitchen and he wasn't there. So it's easy for him to slip in and out of the kitchen. Motive would be by killing Temperance he'd be guaranteed to keep his restaurant."

"But I didn't see him wearing any glitter," Raven said.

58

I yawned and rubbed my eyes.

"I'll take over." Peyton grabbed the notebook from me. "Brandon's dad, Mr. Powell. I *really* hope it's not him."

"That boy is so gaga over you," Raven said. "He could hardly form a complete sentence in your presence tonight."

Peyton blushed. "Oh, that's not true. Is it?"

I snorted. "So totally true. He likes you."

Peyton smiled shyly. "He *is* cute. Although he's like a whole year younger than me."

"Um," Raven said, "plus his dad may be a killer. So you might not want to rush into anything too serious."

I tried not to laugh, but I couldn't help it. "There is that."

"Shut up!" Peyton said with a laugh. "Both of you just shut up."

I grinned at Raven then motioned for Peyton to continue.

She cleared her throat and read from the notebook. "He has an eviction notice from Temperance, and he came to the party to talk with her. We know he left before the body was discovered, but it seemed like he was in a really big hurry to leave minutes before the discovery. Motive to kill would be he gets to keep a roof over his family's head." She checked off his name. "And last but not least we have Thomas and Beatrice Baskins."

"Which I hope it's not," I said. "I'd hate to see the diner close."

Peyton threw a pillow at me.

"What?" I asked. "I'm just being truthful."

"According to the wife," Peyton said primly, "Thomas has been in love with Temperance for years."

Raven made a gagging noise, and I giggled.

Peyton's nostrils flared. "I'm trying to be serious here. Anyway, Thomas is in love with Temperance, but I don't really think the motive is strong."

"I don't either," I said. "He's really not gaining anything by killing her. Maybe he did it out of jealousy, but that's it. He doesn't inherit money, get to stay in a house, nothing like that."

"What about the wife?" Raven asked. "She has a better motive."

"Right," I agreed. "Beatrice was jealous of Temperance, and while she may not have gained anything like the others as far as motive, she did have an incentive to kill. Maybe by getting rid of Temperance, her husband would then love her."

"That's so sad," Peyton said.

"And it could be just like I outlined earlier," Raven said, "but instead of Mariah entering the library, it was Beatrice."

"I agree." I stretched and got under the covers. "Is that everyone we need to get alibis for tomorrow?"

Raven dropped the notebook onto the floor and crawled under the covers on her side of the bed. "Yep."

"Hand me my pillow I threw at you," Peyton said. "I need it back."

I tossed the pillow down to her and she tucked it under her head and pulled an extra blanket up around her, settling in at the foot of the bed.

"Thank goodness you have a king-sized bed," Raven murmured. "Otherwise, it would be really crowded."

I smiled and turned off the lamp, plunging us into darkness. A few seconds later, I felt Jinx walk across the length of my body and settle in next to my head. Purring, he laid his head next to my ear and lulled me into sleep.

CHAPTER 10

"So what's on your agenda today?" Grams asked as she slid a massive stack of pancakes onto the table.

I immediately speared two and plopped them down on my plate. "We're gonna go get some alibis."

Grams sighed. "I figured. And I suppose I'm just wasting my breath when I say maybe you should let the police take care of this?"

"Yep, sure are." I smothered my pancakes in syrup then took a huge bite. "We're doing this for Aunt Aggie."

Grams scoffed and crossed her arms over her chest. "You're doing no such thing."

Peyton and Raven kept their heads down and didn't say a word. The traitors.

"What can you tell me about Temperance?" I asked. "Was she ever married to Percy's dad?"

"Yes. He died about ten years ago in a car accident."

"Was he the rich one or did she always have the money?" I asked.

"Temperance's parents were middle class. She went away to college and came back married to a wealthy man from San Francisco. They had the big house built right before she had Percy."

"I know she said she was part of the original founding families in Copper Cove," I said.

Grams frowned and sat down at the table. "That's true. I believe their last name was Graffman, if memory serves."

"No other family members outside of Percy that will inherit?" Peyton asked.

"Nope. Percy was an only child."

I kissed Grams goodbye and promised we'd stop in at the apothecary later to let her know how things were going. Jinx was waiting by the door.

"You can't go with us," I said. "You need to keep Grams company at the store today."

Meow! Jinx flicked his tail in annoyance.

"Don't be like that, Jinx," I said. "We've got serious business to take care of today."

Without a word, Jinx turned his back on me and started to groom himself. I walked out onto the porch and immediately saw Chief Baedie back out of Aunt Aggie's driveway.

"C'mon," I said. "Let's go see Aunt Aggie."

We raced across the street and inside the house, taking Aunt Aggie by surprise.

"Did you give him the list?" I asked.

"I did," Aunt Aggie said. "And it looked like he was particularly interested in two people." She laughed. "Well, two others *besides* me."

I rolled my eyes. "He's ridiculous."

"Who were his main suspects?" Raven asked. "Could you tell?"

"He already caught word about the man that came here looking for Temperance about being evicted," Aunt Aggie said. "So I know he's on the short list. And then when he saw Mariah Lawson helped cater last night, he really seemed to zero in on her."

"I figured he'd latch onto Mariah easily enough," I said. "I think we have a couple other suspects that are stronger than Mr. Powell."

Aunt Aggie nodded. "If you girls need any help, let me know."

We jogged back across the street and piled into Raven's car. I didn't have a car because you really didn't needed one in Copper Cove. You could pretty much get anywhere in town by walking. But Raven's dad gave her a really cool car that not only he drove, but *his* dad drove. It was a '66 Mustang Fastback. And boy could it fly.

"So what's the plan?" Raven asked as she got behind the wheel of her car. "Are we doing the flowers routine like we did before?"

Last month when sleuthing, I got the bright idea to use Peyton's employment at her dad's funeral home to sneak in to a couple suspects' houses.

"Not this time," I said. "I think we just play it straight. I say we go to Percy's door and ask to be seen."

Peyton settled into the backseat. "You think that'll work?"

I shrugged. "Percy seems like a decent guy. I don't think he'll throw us out."

One of the great things about living in a small town was that you pretty much knew where everyone lived. It was definitely true for Temperance Clairmont. Her house was two miles out of town and was a mansion. And I'm not exaggerating one bit. It was a literal mansion.

"Wow," Raven whispered. "It's gorgeous."

The house overlooked the Pacific Ocean and had to be at least five thousand square feet. It was bright white with huge pillars in the front, a wraparound porch, and a ton of windows.

Raven parked in the circle drive, and I knocked on the front door. After a couple seconds, I rang the doorbell. Probably the house was so huge you couldn't hear a knock.

A man dressed in a fancy tux opened the door. "May I help you?"

"Hi. My name is Brynn O' Connell, and this is Peyton Patterson and Raven Masters. We'd like to see Percy and Barbie."

"Are they expecting you?" the man asked.

"Maybe," I hedged. "We were at the same party last night where Mrs. Clairmont died. And we'd like to offer our condolences."

"Is that so?"

"Look, the party was at my aunt's house," I said, "and she asked me to come see how they were doing."

He sighed and nodded. "Very well. You may come inside, but wait right here, and I will see if Mr. Clairmont and his fiancée are entertaining guests this morning."

"I hope they aren't entertaining," Raven snickered when the butler left, "that would be so wrong."

I let out a little whistle as I looked around the massive foyer. "I thought the B&B was impressive. It doesn't have anything on this house."

A curved, oak staircase led to the upstairs. On the walls leading up were large portraits of older people. It reminded me of those portraits that changed up in Harry Potter.

"Mr. Clairmont and Miss Barbie will see you," the butler said as he ambled slowly into the foyer. "Please follow me. They are still eating breakfast."

We followed him through the foyer and down a hallway that opened to a large sitting area. We crossed that room and took a left and went through another doorway which emptied into the dining room. Percy and Barbie were sitting at a ten-person table eating their breakfast.

"Company!" Barbie exclaimed as she set her drink down on the table. "Look honey, it's the girls from last night."

Percy sighed and set down his coffee cup. "I'm aware. Johnson came to tell us they were here, remember?"

Barbie giggled. "Oh yeah."

Looking at Barbie, I had to wonder if she was for real. Today she had on a midnight blue beaded sparkly dress...like she was ready to go to a fancy ball. Her hair was in an elaborate twist on top of her head, and her makeup was perfect.

"There's coffee on the buffet over there," Percy said. "Help yourselves."

"No thanks," Peyton said. "We just stopped by to say we're sorry for your loss."

Percy looked at Peyton and frowned. "Your dad owns the funeral home in town, right? He's the one that worked on..." he trailed off.

"Your mom?" Peyton supplied. "Yes, he is."

"I believe I have an appointment with him later today to discuss arrangements," Percy said.

"After you meet with the family lawyer that is," Barbie giggled.

66

Percy scowled at Barbie, but if she caught the look, she didn't act like it bothered her.

"I guess Chief Baedie hasn't had time to stop by this morning yet?" I asked.

"Yes," Percy said. "He stopped by about an hour ago to ask me who I thought might want to hurt my mother."

"And of course we told him we didn't know of a single person who would want to hurt Momma Temperance," Barbie added.

Percy took a sip of his coffee. "Then he said he was headed into town to your aunt's house to get the list of guests who attended the party last night."

I frowned. "What? Seriously? Chief Baedie didn't go over your alibis?"

"Our alibis?" Barbie gasped. "Why would we need an alibi?"

"Yes," Percy said. "We don't need alibis. I would never hurt my mother. Neither would Barbie."

I glared at Barbie, but she chose that moment to take a huge drink of her coffee and didn't meet my eye.

"You both had a motive to kill her," Raven said.

"You," I said, pointing to Percy, "are going to inherit a ton of money. Plus, you won't have your mom dictating your life and telling you what to do."

"And you," Peyton added, turning to a shocked Barbie, "won't have to worry about signing that prenup."

Barbie waved her hand in the air. "I never really worried about that. Honest."

I snorted. "Really? Then what was that fight about in the side yard last night...minutes before Mrs. Clairmont was found?"

"What? What fight?" Percy's face was red as he pushed back from the table and stood. "What're they talking about? I thought you told Chief Baedie you didn't go into the library because the door was closed and instead you went to the restroom?"

Barbie's eyes widened and her mouth trembled. "I did. I mean, I—that's exactly what happened. I never stepped foot in the library."

I bit my lip, unsure if I should pull out the rhinestone now and demand to see the dress, or if I should wait for a better time...like after we had more physical evidence against her.

"You're lying," I said to Barbie. "The three of us saw you. You went to the library, maybe saw Temperance there, and somehow you two stepped outside via the French doors in the library, because we saw the door still open. You two had words, and Temperance went back inside the library. You hurled your glass of champagne against a tree and stalked back inside the house."

"I don't know what you're talking about," Barbie said. "I went to the restroom and then met back up with you all in the great room while we waited for Momma Temperance to come back from the library."

"It's not just us that saw you arguing," I said. "When you threw your drink, you almost hit someone with it. We went over and talked with them about what had happened."

Barbie stuck a finger in her mouth and started nibbling on her nail. "Fine! You caught me. I did have words with Momma Temperance, but I didn't kill her." She stuck out her lower lip in a pout. "Percy, honey, you know I love you and loved Momma Temperance. I'd *never* hurt her."

Percy closed his eyes and rubbed his temple. "Look, I have to meet with my attorney in half an hour. Then go to the funeral home and take care of arrangements. We're done here. If Barbie or I answer any more questions, it will be from Chief Baedie or one of his men. Not a bunch of snooping kids. You need to go."

"Yeah." Barbie stood and rushed over to Percy. "You need to go. We have mourning things we need to see to."

Mourning things? Oh, brother!

"Let's go girls," I said. "I think we have everything."

"I'll walk you out," Barbie said. "This house is so big a person could get lost."

We followed her out to the foyer, but when I went to open the door, Barbie grabbed my arm.

"Look here, you little brats," she hissed, "I didn't kill that old hag, so stop telling Percy I did."

"You're gonna want to let go of Brynn," Raven said quietly.

"Oh yeah?" Barbie sneered. "Why's that?"

"Because I'm a blackbelt," Raven said. "I could kick your butt with both of my hands tied behind my back. And I'd sure hate to mess up your pretty hairdo."

Barbie dropped my arm and patted down her hair. "Get out, and don't come back!"

CHAPTER 11

"Wow," Peyton said as she climbed into the backseat of the Mustang, "that woman is crazy. Although I'll feel sorry for Percy if we discover Barbie *did* kill Temperance. He'll have lost both women in his life."

"He'd be better off," Raven said.

I reached out with both hands and yanked the door closed. I always had a hard time shutting the long, heavy door. "Of the two, I think Barbie is the stronger suspect. I'm not dismissing Percy, but I'm leaning more towards Barbie."

"We also need to figure out a way to see if that rhinestone came from her dress," Raven said.

"I'm more concerned about the fact Chief Baedie once again isn't doing his job right," I said. "Does he *seriously* not consider either of them suspects? That's just ridiculous."

"Him being the chief is ridiculous," Raven said.

We'd just entered the city limits when Peyton leaned up from the backseat and pointed out the windshield. "Hey look! Isn't that Brandon?"

Twenty yards ahead of us Brandon held the hand of a little girl as they walked down Main street. Raven slowed and pulled over to the side of the road.

I manually rolled down the window and leaned out. "Hey, Brandon. What's up?"

Brandon and a little girl both turned around and stared at us. He smiled when he recognized us, but the little girl wrapped her arms around his legs and hid behind him. Brandon reached down and smoothed her hair.

"Jillian and I are just out walking around," Brandon said.

"I want to get my daddy a Christmas present," Jillian said. "I have a dollar."

Brandon smiled down at his sister. "Also, Chief Baedie stopped by to ask D-A-D some questions, and D-A-D thought I should take Jillian for a walk."

"I can spell you know!" The little girl rolled her eyes at her brother. "I'm in kindergarten now."

"Right," Brandon said. "My bad, Jillian."

"Why don't you hop in," I said, "and we'll stop by the apothecary. I may have just the thing for your dad."

"The what?" Jillian asked.

I opened the door. "Trust me."

Brandon cleared his throat. "Not that I don't appreciate it, but isn't that mostly medicines and girlie stuff?"

I got out of the car and tipped the seat up so they could get in the back with Peyton. "I actually make a soap that's perfect for deep sea divers and fishermen."

They got in the backseat, and a few minutes later Raven parked outside Grams' store. I looked over across the street and suddenly remembered about Brandon needing a part-time job. I made a mental note for us to stop by Sisters after shopping and kill two birds with one stone.

"It smells really good in here," Jillian said as we walked inside the apothecary.

"Thank you," Grams said from behind the counter. "It's one of the things I aim for."

Meow!

Merriment & Murder

"Kitty!" Jillian dropped down to her knees, scooped up Jinx, and gave him a big hug.

I tried not to laugh at the petrified look on the cat's face.

"Be gentle," Brandon said. "You don't want to hurt the kitty."

"I know," Jillian said.

We left Jillian on the floor playing with Jinx and headed over to where Grams stood. There were about four other customers in the shop, but they weren't paying us any attention.

"So what's new?" Grams asked.

I leaned over the counter so no one could overhear. "We went to see Percy and Barbie this morning, and they basically told us that Chief Baedie told them they weren't suspects."

"The fool!" Grams exclaimed. "I swear that man wouldn't know a viable suspect or a clue if it came up and bit him on the butt."

"But the chief did come by our house," Brandon said quietly. "That's why Jillian and I are out. Dad didn't want Jillian to overhear anything."

"What kind of vibe did you get?" I asked.

"I only overheard a little," Brandon said. "But it sounds like Chief Baedie thinks my dad is the killer."

"Oh no," Peyton said. "That's horrible."

"I don't know what to do," Brandon said. "If they arrest my dad, someone will come and take Jillian and me away."

"We won't let it come to that," Peyton said. "Will we, Brynn?"

Oh boy!

72

"No, we sure won't," I said. Even though I wasn't sure I felt as adamant about Mr. Powell's innocence as Peyton.

"And if it does come down to your dad being arrested," Raven said, "I'll call in my dad. He's a great defense attorney."

Grams nodded. "He kept my keister out of jail last month."

"What's your dad's alibi?" I asked. "What happened after he had words with Temperance and he left the parlor last night?"

"I don't know," Brandon said. "I walked around looking for him and finally found him in that little room off the dining room. All white room with Christmas lights up. Dad was staring out into nothing. I was scared."

"Did he say anything?" I asked.

"Just that he tried to talk again with Temperance, but her son made him go away. We really just hung out in that room for quite a while, trying to come up with ways to get the money. It was peaceful out there, with only the Christmas lights and candles."

"Then what happened?" Raven asked.

"I'd say we'd been out there for about fifteen minutes when this woman comes out. She was really upset. She stood on the other side of the room staring into her coffee. She had on some kind of sparkly sweater. Christmas trees, I think."

"Beatrice," I murmured.

"Anyway, this guy came in and got pretty mean with her. Told her to get her stuff around he was ready to leave, and she asked him if it was because Temperance was getting ready to leave too." Brandon frowned and shook his head.

"He was really mad at her. Told her to grow up and then left her there."

"What did she do?" I asked.

"She hid her face behind her hair and wiped at her eyes. I wanted to ask her if she was okay, but I didn't want to embarrass her. And Dad put his hand on my arm and shook his head. I guess he didn't want me to say anything, either. Then she just wiped away her tears, stood up, and walked away. I didn't see where she went after that."

"Then what happened?" Peyton asked.

Brandon flushed and let out a shaky laugh. "Then Dad and I went to the dining room and started shoving a ton of cookies in our jacket pockets before we turned to leave. We made it to the foyer before someone Dad knew stopped to talk with him for a few minutes."

"We must have *just* missed you guys," I said. "Because we went through that same room to go outside and gather wood for the fireplace."

"But the timeline sounds right," Raven said.

"Did you see anything out of the ordinary while you were in the hallway waiting on your dad?" I asked.

Brandon looked up toward the ceiling. "Not really. There were still people hanging out in the foyer and side hallway. Others were walking back and forth between the rooms." He stopped. "Wait. I think I did see that one lady who was with Mrs. Clairmont go into the library."

"Who?" I asked. "What did she look like?"

He slid a glance at Peyton. "Tall, blonde hair. Kinda pretty. Was in this red sparkly dress that could blind a person every time she walked."

74

"Barbie," Peyton, Raven, and I said simultaneously.

I looked Brandon in the eye. "This is important, Brandon. Was your dad out of your sight at all during the time you saw Barbie go into the library and you waved goodbye to us on the lawn?"

Brandon's face fell. "Yes. I told Dad I wanted to go back and get Jillian some more gingerbread men. I left him in the foyer talking with someone by the library there and went back to the dining room."

Darn!

"But I wasn't gone long," Brandon said. "I promise. It was just quick enough to go grab Jillian some more gingerbread men and go outside."

"I liked the gingerbread men," Jillian said.

We all glanced down at the girl in surprise. None of us had heard her or Jinx move over to us. Jinx jumped up onto the counter and ran his head into my hand. Taking the hint, I reached under his chin and scratched his neck.

"Can I smell that soap I want for my daddy?" Jillian asked.

"Right this way," I said. "I have a lot of soaps I make, but this one is special for men like your daddy who get sea salt on them."

I took her by the area where I kept my products. I had soaps, lotions, body scrubs, and even a few natural cosmetics customers could choose from. Handing her a brown bar of soap, I explained to her it was a pine tar soap.

"It smells weird," Jillian said.

"I know. But it works."

Jillian grinned. "How much? Will my dollar be enough?"

I pursed my lip. "Tell ya what. I'll give you the Christmas special. It's two for one today. You can have two bars for your one dollar."

"Thanks!" She reached out and hugged my waist as I grab another pine tar soap from the tub.

"Thank you," Brandon said. "I know you took a hit on that."

"It's no problem." I walked back and laid my dollar on the counter for Grams to put in the till. "We're gonna run across the street to Sisters real quick. I want Jessica and Janice to meet Brandon. They're looking for a part-time worker."

"Today?" Brandon asked. "But I got my sister with me. I can't do an interview today."

"Pfft." I waved my hand in the air. "They aren't going to care. C'mon, before someone else applies for the job."

"Then where are you amateur sleuthers off to?" Grams asked.

"I want to stop by Aunt Aggie's place," I said. "I think Chef Granger is a suspect."

Grams snorted. "Don't let your aunt hear that. She's always had a thing for Jimmy. Clear back in school."

CHAPTER 12

We waved goodbye and headed across the street. The bakery and coffee shop was packed, which was no surprise. It took us ten minutes before we reached the counter to place our orders.

"Good afternoon," Jessica chirped. "What can I get for you all?"

"Triple shot mocha for me," I said.

"Same," Raven and Peyton echoed.

"And for you two?" Jessica asked.

Brandon backed up. "Oh, nothing for us. Thanks."

Jillian tugged on Brandon's coat. "I want something."

Brandon gave us a wan smile before kneeling down to Jillian's level. "We can't today. Okay. I promise I'll bring you in another time."

"You know," Jessica said, "I *did* just make up a batch of hot chocolate that I'm not sure is any good. Would you two like to try that and see what you think?"

Jillian's eyes grew wide. "Can we?"

Jessica nodded to Brandon. "We can do that if it's okay."

"Thanks." Brandon leaned in closer to the counter. "I was kind of hoping to talk with you about the job opening."

Jessica clapped her hands together. "Wonderful. Give me a second to get these drinks around, and then Janice and I can talk with you for a second while the other workers man the counter."

We sat at a six-person table and made small talk while we waited for our drinks. About five minutes later, Jessica set down a tray of our drinks while Janice placed a tray of baked goodies on the table.

"Can we eat those?" Jillian asked.

"You sure can," Janice said. "I needed to make some space in the display case, so I thought maybe you guys would take these off my hand."

Before Brandon could say anything to Jillian, the little girl reached out and snatched a chocolate donut and shoved it in her mouth. He laughed and handed her a napkin.

"So you're interested in the job?" Jessica asked.

Brandon and the twins spent a few minutes going over the details of the job, while I contemplated our next move, sipped coffee, and munched donuts.

"Thanks," Brandon said. "I really appreciate it."

I shook myself out of my fog and focused in on the conversation.

"We heard about what happened last night," Janice said. "We'd already left the party."

"Do the police have suspects in mind, do you know?" Jessica asked.

I slid a glance at Brandon, but before I could say anything, Raven took out her cell phone and groaned.

"What is it?" Peyton asked.

Raven looked at Brandon. "It's my dad. He said he's heard through the lawyer grapevine that they are bringing in two people for formal questioning later today."

"Did he say who?" Brandon whispered.

Raven plunked out a text and hit send. A few seconds later she got a reply. She didn't even have to say it aloud, I could tell by the look on her face.

"One of them is your dad," Raven said.

"Something serious must have come up during their talk this morning," Peyton said. "Something that required a trip to the station."

"Oh no," Jessica said. "There has to be a mistake. I've known Scott Powell my whole life—Janice and I both have—there's no way he'd do that."

"What's the matter, Brandon?" Jillian asked.

"Nothing," he soothed. "Drink your cocoa. We need to leave in a few minutes."

"I bet the other person being taken in for a formal interview is Mariah," I said.

Raven's phone rang. She stood up and walked away to answer it. I looked at Brandon, unsure of what to say.

"We'll figure this out," Peyton said. "Don't worry."

Raven sat down at the table. "I explained to Dad what was going on. He wanted me to ask you if you guys have a family attorney or know of someone. If not, he'd be more than happy to go down to the station."

Brandon shook his head. "We don't know any attorneys. Heck, we can't afford an attorney."

"Give me your number, and I'll give it to my dad so he can call your dad." Raven sent the number and message a few seconds later.

"What's going on, Brandon?" Jillian asked, her face covered in chocolate.

Brandon handed her a napkin. "Wipe your mouth, Jilly. It's nothing for you to worry about. But we need to get home."

"I'll drive you," Raven said.

"No. I want to give Dad a little space. We can walk."

My heart hurt as Jillian and Brandon headed out the door toward home. I knew just how he felt. I went through the same thing a month ago with Grams. I had no idea how I was going to survive, and it was just me. He had a little sister to think about.

"Anything we can do," Jessica said, "you let us know."

"Will do," I said.

Strolling back outside, we crossed the street and got into the Mustang. I wasn't sure if we should go see Aunt Aggie next or Mariah. I was trying to time it so we wouldn't run into Chief Baedie.

"Let's go see what Aunt Aggie knows," I said. "Then we can follow up with Mariah, Beatrice, and Thomas."

The front door to the B&B was unlocked, so I let us in and headed to the back of the house.

"Aunt Aggie?"

"Back here, Brynn," she called out.

Aunt Aggie and Chef Granger were standing in the middle of the kitchen eating sandwiches.

"Grilled cheese," Chef Granger said. "You girls want one?"

"You're like this famous chef," I said. "Why're you making grilled cheese?"

Chef Granger grinned. "These aren't your typical grilled cheese. Trust me."

"I'll take one," Raven said.

"Me too," Peyton said.

My mouth dropped open. "We just had donuts."

"And now I need something to soak up all that sugar and caffeine," Raven said.

I shrugged. "Makes sense, I guess. I'll have one too."

Chef Granger turned to the stove and started preparing our meal. "Do you guys like avocados?"

"Yes. But on a grilled cheese?" I scoffed. "Yuck."

"Just trust me," he said.

"So how's it going so far?" Aunt Aggie asked. "Anything promising?"

I slid a glance at Chef Granger. "We're still tracking down alibis."

"Who all have you talked with this morning?" Aunt Aggie asked.

"Percy and Barbie," Peyton said. "Plus we've gotten Mr. Powell's alibi."

I cleared my throat. "We still have Mariah, Thomas, and Beatrice to talk with. And then..."

"And then?" Aunt Aggie prompted.

Chef Granger turned from the stove. "Me?"

Aunt Aggie's mouth dropped. "You? Why you?"

CHAPTER 13

"I wondered if you'd overheard the conversation between Temperance and myself," Chef Granger said. "I guess you did."

Aunt Aggie held up a hand. "Wait. What's going on here, James?"

"Peyton, Raven, and I were in the butler's pantry last night sneaking cookies," I said. "We were about to head back into the party when we heard someone arguing."

"Temperance had stopped me to let me know if I didn't fire Mariah immediately she was going to call a bank board meeting on Monday and demand they call in my loan payment."

"Why take it out on you?" Aunt Aggie asked.

Chef Granger sighed. "It's more than just me hiring Mariah. Last year, I dated Temperance for a very short time. Not even a month."

I bit my lip to keep from laughing at the incredulous look Aunt Aggie gave him.

"She was quite a bit younger than us in school," Aunt Aggie said, "so I really didn't know her that well. But from what I saw last night, she hadn't changed much."

"It didn't take me long to see her true colors," Chef Granger said. "I broke it off as soon as I figured out her game. She was a very manipulative woman. Downright mean."

"I think we were the only ones to overhear the conversation," I said. "So you shouldn't really be on Chief

Baedie's radar. But you understand why we need to ask you where you were at certain times last night, right?"

Chef Granger nodded. "I do. And I respect the fact you're asking."

"The truth is, I don't know if you were in the kitchen or not when she was killed," I said. "I know for a fact there were a few times when we walked through the kitchen last night and you weren't there. And one of the last times anyone saw Temperance alive was right before we went to gather wood, and you were in the kitchen talking with Mariah."

"I *was* in and out of the kitchen at all hours last night. And after you girls went through the kitchen to go outside, and Mariah and I parted company, I think I did go into the dining room to check on the cookie supply. However, when I heard about Temperance's discovery, I *was* in the kitchen. It was Mariah who came and got me."

"Did you kill Temperance Clairmont?" Raven asked.

"I did not."

He handed me a plate, and I set it down on the counter. Peyton and Raven accepted their sandwiches and began devouring them. Following suit, I picked up the grilled cheese and took a big bite.

"Oh my gosh," I moaned. "This is amazing."

"It sure is," Raven agreed.

"Don't take this the wrong way," I said, "but we really can't just take you on your word you didn't kill her."

James grinned. "You're a tough nut to crack."

There was a lull before Aunt Aggie spoke. "I've known James for a good number of years. Granted, we lost touch for a significant period of time, but I have to go on faith that if he says he didn't kill Temperance, then he didn't kill her."

I gave him my best steely look. "I will admit I have stronger suspects. But if after we question Thomas and Beatrice we feel they aren't viable candidates, I'm going to have to circle back to you. You understand that, right?"

Chef Granger nodded. "I do. But I can promise you, I didn't kill her."

Aunt Aggie stood up. "You girls finish up. I have to go back to cleaning. You can tell it's Christmas...glitter everywhere."

I snorted. "Yeah, not sure when the last time I saw so much glitter. Even Jessica and Janice had on glitter dresses last night."

"I've had to dump my vacuum six times already," Aunt Aggie said. "And I've only done the great room and front parlor. I can't tackle the library until Chief Baedie gives me the go-ahead it's okay to enter."

Aunt Aggie walked out of the kitchen, leaving us alone with Chef Granger.

"Did I tell you my grandson is moving to Copper Cove next week?" he asked. "He'll start high school after the new year."

"What grade?" Raven asked.

"Senior," Chef Granger said.

"What?" I exclaimed. "Who starts a new school the last semester of their senior year?"

"My son is a police officer," Chef Granger said. "He applied for the officer position here in Copper Cove a few weeks ago and got the job."

I knew exactly what job opening he was talking about, and why it was open. "Your grandson isn't upset that he has to move to a different school his senior year?"

"No. His mother passed away a few years ago, and it's just been him and his dad. My grandson already has his life planned out. He's going into the Marine Corps after he graduates, and he's already said it doesn't matter to him what school he graduates from as long as he graduates."

I crossed my arms over my chest and stared Chef Granger in the eyes. "Then I guess it's a good thing you didn't kill Temperance. I'd hate to think your son would have to arrest you for murder his first week on the job."

Chef Granger grinned. "I knew I liked you for a reason."

CHAPTER 14

"How much farther?" Raven asked.

We were on our way to talk with Mariah. I didn't think it would be cool to ask Chef Granger to rat out his worker with her address, so I pulled her name up on the internet and found her address. I recognized the street name, so all we had to do was find the right house.

"Look!" Peyton exclaimed from the backseat. "Isn't that Percy?"

"Slow down! Slow down!" I said to Raven.

Pulling over to the side of the street, we watched as Mariah waved goodbye to Percy. He pulled out of her driveway, never once looking our way.

"I thought he was going to see his lawyer," Peyton said, "and then going to the funeral home."

Raven snorted. "Guess he forgot to tell Barbie of his plans."

"Omigosh!" I said. "Do you guys think maybe they're in this together?"

"You mean like the two of them planned it beforehand?" Peyton asked.

"Could be," Raven said. "I mean, Mariah obviously knew she was going to be working the event, so there's opportunity. She and Percy devise a plan to take out his mom. He inherits, she marries him, everyone is happy."

"Except Temperance," I said. "She's dead. She ain't happy."

"I don't know," Peyton said. "Mariah looked miserable last night when she saw Percy and Barbie together. If Percy

86

and Mariah planned it ahead of time, they sure are convincing."

"And besides," Raven added, "they couldn't have planned ahead of time to kill Temperance in the library when she was in there, because they'd have no idea Temperance would be in there alone. This was impulsive. The killer saw an opportunity and took it."

I sighed. "You're right. I guess I got carried away."

"What *does* stick out," Raven said, "is the fact that now that Temperance is out of the picture, Mariah can have what she wants. And from the looks of it, she's going to get it."

We waited a few more minutes to let Mariah settle back down inside before I knocked on her door.

"This is a surprise," she said, glancing in the direction Percy's car had just driven off in. "What's going on?"

"We just came to see how you were doing," I lied. "Aunt Aggie said when Chief Baedie left her house this morning, he had you in his sights. How're you holding up?"

Emotion flickered in her eyes...I couldn't be sure if it was anger or fear. "Yes, the Chief did stop by."

"Everything okay?" Peyton asked.

"No," she snapped, "everything is not okay. I have to go down to the station for a formal interview in about an hour."

I shrugged. "But he doesn't really have anything on you. Right?"

Mariah narrowed her eyes. "Of course he doesn't. I didn't do anything."

I scrunched up my face, pretending to think. "I mean, outside of the fact you and Percy used to be engaged, he doesn't have anything." I paused. "Well, and the fact you were wearing a glittery shirt and there was glitter found on Temperance's body. But that's all, right?"

"I didn't kill Temperance Clairmont, and I don't have to prove otherwise."

"Unless you're arrested," Raven said. "Then you might want to."

Mariah snorted. "I'm not getting arrested. Chief Baedie said this was just a question and answer session in an ongoing investigation."

Raven clucked her tongue. "I hate to tell you this, Mariah, but with both of my parents being lawyers, I know standard cop speak for number one suspect when I hear it."

The color drained from Mariah's face, and I hoped like heck she was guilty...otherwise I was gonna feel bad for making her sweat the interview.

"I overheard what Temperance said to you by the staircase," I said, "right before she went to the library to retrieve the book she was looking for."

"You did?"

Nodding, I gave her my most sympathetic smile. "I did. I'm sorry for what she said to you. And then a few minutes later, the three of us cut through the kitchen and saw you and Chef Granger. You looked like you'd been crying."

"Look, I may have been upset, but I wasn't upset enough to follow her into the library and murder her."

"Don't take this the wrong way," I said, "but right before she died, you said to her you hoped she choked on all the bad things she ever said about you. And then moments later, someone strangles her. You understand how that looks, right?"

88

Mariah took a step back into her house. "Chief Baedie has asked me to bring in my t-shirt from last night when I go in for the interview. He said if I didn't do it voluntarily, he could get a search warrant. I don't know what he is hoping to find, but he won't find it on my shirt...because I didn't kill her."

CHAPTER 15

"Hopefully we'll learn something more from Thomas or Beatrice," Peyton said.

"Luckily with us being on Christmas vacation," I said, "we can investigate tomorrow if we need to."

Raven turned onto Fishermen's Drive and continued down the narrow street. Houses were lined on both sides of the road, and Christmas decorations were up on most houses.

"Look." I pointed to Thomas Baskins high on a ladder stringing Christmas lights on his house. "Hope this means Beatrice is home too."

Raven pulled into the drive and we headed over to Thomas. He scowled down at us from the top of the ladder.

"I've already heard through the grapevine about you girls," he said. "When your grandmother was arrested last month, you three went on a mission to prove her innocence. I don't know what you're doing here, but I'm sure it has to do with Temperance's death."

His voice caught on Temperance's name, but I pretended not to notice. "We'd just like to talk with Beatrice for a minute."

"Beatrice is sick," Thomas said. "She's too ill to speak to you today."

The front door opened, and I turned to look at Beatrice. He hadn't been exaggerating...Beatrice looked like death. She was pale and sweaty, and swaying lightly on her feet.

"I thought I heard voices out here."

Her speech had a slight slur to it.

"You girls come in now." She gestured weakly for us to follow her.

"Not long," Thomas said. "Beatrice, you need your rest to feel better."

She nodded slowly and then shut the door behind us.

"What's wrong?" I asked. "You didn't seem sick last night."

She touched her temple and smiled. "It was sudden. I felt okay when I went to bed, but this morning after breakfast, I just felt horrible. I'm hoping it's just a twenty-four hour flu bug. I can't afford to be sick right now. We're busy at the diner, and I have Christmas to get ready for next week."

"Let's sit down," Peyton said. "You look like you could fall over any minute now."

"You girls are so sweet."

We followed her into the living room and sat down.

"We're just stopping by people's houses this morning," I said, "and making sure everyone is all right after what happened last night."

"A lot of people are sad over Temperance's death," Raven said.

I tried not to snort at her obvious lie.

"I'm not," Beatrice said. "I'm glad she's dead."

I reached out and patted her hand. "Yeah, you did seem a little upset last night."

Beatrice blinked back tears. "She was a horrible woman. She got what she deserved." Beatrice put her hand to her head again. "Or is it she deserved what she got? My mind seems to be a little foggy right now."

Peyton scooted to the edge of the couch and leaned forward to catch Beatrice's eyes. "My friend, Brandon, said he saw you in the conservatory, and that you looked upset."

Beatrice frowned. "I guess so."

"He was going to talk with you," Peyton continued, "but he said Thomas came in and said he was ready to go. You two had words and then you left the room."

"Yes," she said. "I think that sounds right."

"Do you remember where you went when you left the room?" I asked.

The front door opened and Thomas walked in. "Beatrice, it's time for your medication. I'll get it and bring it to you."

"I'm sorry you're feeling so awful," Peyton said. "Be sure to rest up after we leave."

"I will," Beatrice promised.

"I like your *A Christmas Story* leg lamp," Raven said. "Very retro."

Beatrice laughed softly. "That's Thomas' lamp. He loves that lamp. Last Christmas I had to fight him to put it away until this Christmas."

"You know, my Grams has the apothecary in town," I said. "If you tell me what your exact symptoms are, she might have something to help."

Thomas strode into the living room and handed a cup to Beatrice. "No offense, Brynn, but Beatrice doesn't need any of that hocus pocus crap. She's seriously ill. I haven't seen her this sick...well, not in the two years we've been married."

I was about to tell him it wasn't hocus pocus crap, but then thought better of it. I'd learned a long time ago you can't change some people's minds so why bother trying.

"Drink it all," Thomas said to Beatrice. "It's the vegetable broth I make that you love."

"Thank you, Thomas." Beatrice took a long sip of the broth and smiled at him. "Thomas has been growing his own vegetables for years. This broth is the perfect blend of carrots, celery, onions, mushrooms, and sage."

"Sounds wonderful," Peyton said.

"Has Chief Baedie stopped by today to ask for your alibis last night?" I asked.

Thomas snorted. "No. Why would he?"

I shrugged. "I just figured he was talking with everyone who was at the party last night. He's talked to my aunt twice."

"Again why?" Thomas asked. "She just moved to town. She wouldn't have a reason to kill Temperance."

"No," I said, "but the scarf used to strangle Temperance was my aunt's. Didn't you know?"

Thomas swallowed hard and blinked back tears. "No. I didn't know it was her scarf."

"A scarf?" Beatrice asked. "Yes."

We all turned to stare at Beatrice. Her eyes were glassy, and she looked ready to keel over at any minute.

"My wife obviously isn't feeling well and needs her rest," Thomas said. "If she doesn't improve by tomorrow, I'm going to have to insist she see a doctor. But right now, I need you three to leave and let her rest."

"Yes," Beatrice slurred. "I need to rest."

***

"That was the weirdest thing ever," I said as we drove back toward Grams' house. "And I'm mad I didn't get a chance to see her sweater. If Chief Baedie wants Mariah to bring in her shirt, they must be trying to match the glitter found on Temperance."

"Pretty smart thinking," Peyton said.

"I'm thinking Beatrice knows something," Raven said. "Maybe she saw something or knows more than she's letting on."

"She's so out of it," Peyton said, "there's no telling what's true and what's a lie right now."

I nodded. "We definitely need to get Beatrice alone again soon and see what she knows."

"Am I taking us back to your Grams'?" Raven asked.

"I think so," I said. "We'll rest up, have dinner, and go over our next move."

"I'd say by the suspicious way Thomas and Beatrice were acting," Raven said, "they move to the top of the list, and we can move Chef Granger down."

"Although," Peyton added, "depending on what happens with Mariah's formal questioning and what they find on her t-shirt, maybe they'll arrest her as the killer and we won't have to investigate anymore."

I shook my head. "I don't think so. We need to go back and see Barbie. Or at least see her dress. Find out if the rhinestone we found in the library is a match to her dress, and if there's something that stands out about the glitter on the dress."

CHAPTER 16

Neither Mariah nor Mr. Powell were arrested, so the next morning we dressed in all black, said goodbye to Jinx and Grams, and headed out to the Clairmont mansion to see Barbie. Or rather...to see if the rhinestone in my pocket was a match to her dress from the party.

"Whoa," Raven said as we turned into the long driveway. "I wonder what's going on?"

"Some kind of wake or something maybe?" I suggested.

"Not that I'm aware of," Peyton said. "Dad said the visitation is tomorrow followed immediately by the funeral."

Raven parked behind a pink and yellow van, and we quickly exited the Mustang.

"Isn't that the van that's always parked in front of Trudy's Salon and Day Spa?" I asked.

Raven's nose scrunched. "Is Barbie getting *pampered* a day before the funeral?"

"That's a little weird," Peyton said.

The front door opened and Johnson stepped out. "Ms. Barbie is waiting in the parlor. Once everyone is inside, I'll escort you to her and Mitzi."

"What do we do?" Peyton asked. "He'll recognize us and send us away."

I looked inside the van and smiled. Opening the door, I reached in and grabbed a Trudy's hat from the seat and stuck it on my head. "Peyton, give Raven one of those hair ties you keep around your wrist. If you both wear your hair up and keep your eyes low, Johnson probably won't even notice us. He's not expecting to see us."

"Everyone looks *way* older than us," Peyton said.

Raven shook her head. "Brynn's right. They're in black, we're in black. Their hair is either pulled up or in a hat, so is ours. We can blend."

We tucked our heads down and got in line behind five other ladies carrying in suitcases, stools, and towels. Johnson led us down the hallway, and this time instead of taking a left we went right and entered a massive great room.

Barbie was reclining in a white chaise lounge, champagne in one hand, teacup Yorkie in the other.

"It's about time," she whined. "Mitzi here was getting anxious."

"Yes, Ms. Barbie," one of the ladies said. "We just need a minute to set up and we'll get started."

"Make it fast," Barbie snapped. "I'm in mourning and need to feel better."

We stood off to the side, not wanting to draw attention to ourselves. I wasn't sure why the other ladies didn't seem interested in us, but I was glad they weren't asking questions.

"I already know what we want," Barbie said. "Mitzi and I want Passion Pink toenails, and Mitzi wants a matching pink bow in her hair."

"Yes, ma'am," a brunette woman said as she sat down on a stool next to the chaise. "Will you be wanting a manicure in the same Passion Pink?"

"Of course!" Barbie giggled. "Momma Temperance *hated* the color. I'm going to make sure I'm covered in it." Barbie took a drink from her flute and giggled again. "Then afterward, Mitzi and I are going to need massages to relax before our big day tomorrow."

As the lady on the stool got started on Barbie's toes, another lady stepped up by Barbie's head and started applying a green face mask. Once the mask was in place, the lady placed a cucumber slice over each eye.

I was about to tell the girls to cover me, I was going to slip upstairs to find Barbie's room, when Barbie lifted one of her cucumber slices and pointed to Raven.

"You. Come here."

Raven gave me an "oh crap" look but slowly sauntered over to Barbie.

"Yes?" Raven asked.

Barbie lifted her head off the chaise and stared pointedly at Raven. "Don't I know you?"

"No. This is my first day working at Trudy's Salon and Day Spa."

"Oh," Barbie said. "Well, let's see what kind of a first day you're gonna have. I feel like good things are about to come my way. I want you to call a fortune teller and get her here immediately."

"A fortune teller?" Raven asked. "Seriously? First off, where am I supposed to find one around here?"

"That's not my problem, girl," Barbie snapped. "That's *yours*. Get it for me now, or I'll have to tell your boss to fire you."

I could tell Raven was about to open a can of whoop-butt on her, so I jogged over. "I believe I know someone."

"Whatever," Barbie said. "Just get them here immediately."

"Mitzi is ready for her massage," a blonde woman said to Peyton. "You may start now."

98

Peyton stared at me wide-eyed, but I jerked my head in the direction of the dog. Obviously the salon workers thought we were the massage therapists.

"You'll be fine," I whispered.

Raven and I hurried out of the room and down the hallway, being careful not to run into Johnson. When we reached the foyer, we sprinted up the stairs to the second floor.

"You take the left side," I said, "and I'll take the right."

A few seconds later, Raven hollered she'd found Barbie's room. There was no doubt it was Barbie's room. The walk-in closet doors were open and inside was filled with brightly-colored clothes, at least twenty pairs of high-heeled shoes, and more designer purses than anyone would ever need.

"This is the dress she wore," I said, pointing to a dress hanging in the back of the closet.

"Don't touch it," Raven advised. "Let's see if it's missing a rhinestone."

It was difficult to search without touching, and just when I was about to give up, Raven pointed to a spot near the hem that was obviously missing a jewel. I took the rhinestone out of my pocket and carefully placed it in the space. It was a perfect fit.

"It's a match," Raven said. "We've done it. We've proven that at some point in the night Barbie was in the library."

"At some point *before* the body was discovered," I added. "Which is important. She can't say it fell off when she entered the library when the cops got there because I already had it, and if it *had* fallen off afterward, the cops would have found it when they processed the scene."

"It looks pretty damning for Barbie," Raven said.

"Do you see anything weird about the glitter, though? Something that stands out?"

"No. It just looks like normal glitter on a dress."

"Let's get out of here and go see Chief Baedie," I said.

Raven grinned. "First, Barbie needs a little scare from a certain fortune teller."

I laughed. "You're just awful."

"I know."

I glanced around the closet. "She has some wigs over there."

"Let me see." Raven walked over and picked up a blonde wig. "This is perfect. Hand me that colorful scarf over there and those big hooped earrings. I'm going to see if this dress over here fits."

When Raven turned around a few seconds later, my mouth hit the floor. She looked nothing like the Raven I was used to.

"Let's see what kind of makeup she has," Raven said. "Do this up right."

When we headed back downstairs, I had no idea who the person next to me was. If we'd passed on the street, I'd never have recognized her. At the bottom of the stairs we parted ways...me walking back to the party, while Raven went outside to ring the doorbell.

When I walked inside the room, Peyton gave me a withering glare as she continued to give Mitzi a massage.

When the doorbell rang, I gave Peyton a grin. It was showtime.

"Ms. Barbie," Johnson said as he stepped into the room, "there's a Miss Youra at the door. She says she's expected."

"Is she a fortune teller?" Barbie asked.

Johnson looked over his shoulder at Raven. "I believe so, Ms. Barbie."

"Well, don't just stand there," Barbie snapped, "show her in."

"As you wish," Johnson said. He motioned for Raven to enter the room. "Is there anything else, Ms. Barbie?"

"No. Shoo. Go on. This is a girls celebration day."

I was pretty sure Johnson rolled his eyes.

"Hello!" Raven threw her arms wide, causing the gauzy, multi-colored maxi dress to flow effortlessly. "My name is Youra...Youra Charlatan, and I'm from a teeny tiny village in Bulgaria."

Barbie sat up and clapped her hands. "Bulgaria. I think I know where that is. Isn't it in Georgia or Alabama?"

"Oh, Ms. Barbie, you are *so* smart," Raven cooed.

Barbie gasped. "You know my name?"

Uh...the butler just said it like ten times.

"I know many things," Raven said.

"Hey," Barbie cocked her head to one side, "I think I have a dress just like that."

Raven gasped and touched her heart. "I feel death. Death is here. Has someone recently died?"

"Yes," Barbie said excitedly, completely forgetting about the dress. "My horrible almost mother-in-law, thank goodness."

"You poor thing," Raven said. "I can see you're all torn up about it."

"I am?" Barbie questioned. "I mean, yes, I am. I'm all torn up about it. That's why Mitzi and I are getting our nails done today. We need to be cheered up, don't we baby?"

I couldn't help it. I sneaked a peek at Peyton. She was biting her lips to keep from laughing. The other four ladies in the room were busy packing away their supplies and paying no attention to what was going on in the room. It was almost like they were robots.

Raven paced in front of the fireplace before coming to an abrupt stop. "This was no ordinary death, was it?"

"What do you mean?" Barbie asked.

Raven clasped her neck and started to cough, then she clawed at her throat like she was trying to pull something off. "I can't breathe. Someone is trying to strangle me!"

Barbie screamed. "Momma Temperance? Is that you?"

"Why is this scarf around my neck?" Raven gasped.

"Momma Temperance?" This time Barbie sounded like she was going to cry.

"You were in the library!" Raven yelled, pointing at Barbie. "Why would you lie and say you weren't. I know what you did!"

Barbie stood up and snatched up Mitzi. "How do you know what I told the police?"

"I know what you did!" Raven screeched again. "Why? Why would you do that?"

Barbie's eyes rolled in the back of her head, and she dropped to the floor with a loud thud. Mitzi jumped out of her arms and sprinted from the room, yapping down the hallway. The four women quietly left the room, their arms loaded down with their supplies, never saying a word.

"Well," Raven said, "that was entertaining."

Peyton and I roared with laughter as Raven took a bow.

CHAPTER 17

"Everything we have is circumstantial," Raven said as we crossed the city limits sign back into Copper Cove, "but I definitely think we need to go to the chief. With our story about how we found the rhinestone, and enough hint dropping that we were sure it was the same stone on Barbie's dress, it should be enough to get a search warrant."

"He's going to be *so* mad we kept the rhinestone," I said.

"We didn't know at the time when we picked it up it was pertinent," Raven said. "And that's honest. The fact you forgot to hand it over is unfortunate, but again, he can't be too upset. We just tell him the minute we remembered, we brought it to him."

"If I ever need legal help in the future," I said, "I'm only coming to you to bail me out."

Peyton laughed. "And when you get older and keep stumbling over dead bodies, I'll be there to tell you exactly what happened to them."

"I like it," I said. "We'll be like our own crime-fighting team."

Raven snorted. "I don't exactly see you as a detective. No offense."

I crinkled my nose. "Yeah, you're right. Unless I was a beauty technician during the day and a crime fighter at night."

"Now you're Batwoman?" Raven asked.

I grinned. "Maybe. You never know."

Raven took a right off Main Street onto Seaside Road when something caught my eye. "Look over there. Thomas is helping Beatrice inside the clinic. I guess she's still not feeling well."

"It has to be pretty serious for both of them to be gone from the diner," Peyton said. "At least one of them is there at all times."

Raven turned into the police station, and we hurried inside. The same woman I met last month when I came to speak to Chief Baedie about my Grams' arrest was again sitting behind the front desk.

"Well, if it isn't the young Nancy Drew girls," she said. "What can the Copper Cove Police Department do for you today?"

Ignoring her obvious sarcasm, I stepped forward. "We'd like to see Chief Baedie." I held up my hand. "And before you tell me he's not in, or he's in a meeting, or he can't just come out here and see us on a whim...you need to tell him we have some evidence and knowledge about the Temperance Clairmont murder he needs to see and hear."

The woman frowned but finally picked up her phone. Turning her back to us, she leaned over and whispered into the mouthpiece. When she turned back around and set the phone in the cradle, she was scowling.

"He'll be with you in a moment," she snapped. "Have a seat."

A moment turned into ten minutes, but finally Chief Baedie came shuffling out from the back of the station. He paused in the doorway, hitched up his pants, and stared us down.

"So you got news I need to hear, huh?" he asked.

"Sure do," I said.

He sighed. "Well then come on back, I guess."

We followed him to his office and waited for him to settle into his chair behind his desk. There weren't enough chairs for all of us, so we stood in solidarity in front of him.

"So whaddya got?" he asked. "You have to know I'm busy trying to solve this murder."

I reached into my pocket, pulled out the rhinestone, and set it on his desk.

"What is it?" he asked.

"When you questioned us the night of the murder," I said, "we told you we saw Barbie and Temperance fighting in the side yard."

Chief Baedie waved his hand in the air. "And when I questioned her the next day, she said otherwise. She claims she never entered the library."

"What I forgot to tell you that night when you questioned me was that when the three of us entered the library to find Temperance, Jinx rushed in ahead of us and found this on the floor."

Chief Baedie's face was dangerously purple. "And you're just now bringing this to my attention? I can't *believe* you picked up a clue and kept it. I could have you arrested for tampering and withholding key evidence in this case."

Raven held up her hand. "First off, Chief, at the time it wasn't evidence. The body had not been discovered. It was just something we found on the floor. Then in the excitement of discovering the body, Brynn forgot she had it. You can't fault her for that. When we realized she still had the rhinestone, we came here to give it to you." She crossed her arms and glared at the chief. "If you want to keep yelling, I could go on with my own argument."

Chief Baedie rolled his eyes. "You're just like your parents."

"Thank you," Raven said. "I'll take that as a compliment."

Chief Baedie snorted but didn't say anything else. Glancing down at the rhinestone, he frowned. "Would you say the dress Barbie wore that night had these rhinestones on it?"

"Yes," Peyton said. "It was a red beaded dress with tiny veins of glitter running through it."

The chief's eyes lit up. "Glitter?"

I nodded enthusiastically, knowing Peyton had hit on the key word.

Chief Baedie sighed. "I'll get a warrant to pick up the dress and have Barbie brought in for questioning."

"Yes!" I cried.

"But this is the last time you girls stick your nose in my investigations," Chief Baedie said. "Do you understand me?"

"Of course," I said. "Wouldn't dream of it."

His scowl let me know he didn't believe a word I said. "Go on, get out. I have some phone calls I have to make."

I stood up and walked toward the door. Then turned around. "Chief? I feel I should tell you we have one other suspect in mind too. I don't know if she's on your radar or not, but we believe she should be."

Chief Baedie sighed. "Who?"

"Beatrice Baskins," I said. "She had a fight with her husband at the party over Temperance."

"Beatrice?" Chief Baedie asked. "And was Beatrice wearing a glittery sweater?"

Peyton nodded. "She sure was."

"But you may have to go see her instead of bringing her in for questioning," I added quickly. "We just saw her and Thomas go into the clinic. When we talked with her yesterday, she was really sick."

"Looks like a bad case of the flu," Raven said.

"Beatrice, huh? I'll keep it in mind," Chief Baedie begrudgingly. "But I think you girls are on the right track with Barbie." He gave me a pointed look. "Of course, the only reason Barbie wasn't on my radar was because you snatched up a pretty important clue, and I was working blind."

Yeah, that's the reason.

Chief Baedie waved his hand toward the door. "Go on. I've got work to do if I want to get this search warrant."

Grinning, the three of us hurried down the hallway and out into the cool afternoon air. I glanced over at the clinic and noticed that Thomas' car was gone.

"I'm hungry," Raven said.

I pulled out my cell phone. "It's after two. I say we go by and see if Grams is at her house or Aunt Aggie's house...and we grab some food. Let them know what's going on."

Usually on Sundays and Mondays, Grams only opens the apothecary from ten to two, and then eight to four or five the rest of the week, depending on how busy she was.

"Hey, there's your granny now," Raven said as she pulled into Aunt Aggie's driveway.

108

Grams and Henley Waller were holding hands and walking into Aunt Aggie's house, Jinx close on their heels. It was still weird to see Grams holding hands with a guy...especially Henley. I always thought she didn't care for him, but really she kept her distance because she didn't *want* to care for him.

Aunt Aggie, Grams, Henley, and Jinx were in the kitchen sipping coffee. I immediately headed toward the pot to pour us each a mug. There was a plate of cookies on the table, along with some fruit.

"Well, well," Aunt Aggie said, "look what the cat dragged in."

Meow! Meow!

I laughed. "She didn't mean it *literally,* Jinx."

"What's new?" Grams asked when we carried our drinks to the table and sat down.

Between bites of cookies, I filled them in on what all had transpired, and when I was done, Henley let out a low whistle.

"That's too bad for the Clairmont boy," he said. "His mom was murdered by his fiancée."

"Maybe now I'll be able to clean up the library," Aunt Aggie said.

"Hey Grams," I said, "Beatrice Baskins is really sick. We just saw her being helped inside the clinic by her husband. I told her yesterday we could probably give her something to help alleviate her symptoms."

"What're her symptoms?" Grams asked.

"She was lethargic, sweating, pale, very shaky. She said she couldn't keep anything down."

"She looked awful," Peyton said.

"I'll tell ya what," Grams said. "Run up to the store and get her some elderberry syrup. If she's been to the doctor, I'm sure they gave her something. But everyone should have some elderberry on hand."

"Thanks. I'll run it up to her later tonight. I'm sure she's resting after her appointment."

"While you're still here," Aunt Aggie said, "tomorrow night James has invited all of us out to his restaurant for dinner. You girls included."

I whistled. "Things seem to be going well."

Aunt Aggie's face turned as pink as the tips in her hair. "Well enough."

"And it sounds like it'll be an extra special celebration," Grams said. "If they make the arrest with Barbie, that means the B&B will be open in time for your first guest, Aggie."

Tears filled Aunt Aggie's eyes. "Yeah, I guess so. I can't believe how quickly my life has changed in a month."

Grams reached across the table and clasped Aunt Aggie's hand. "I'm glad you're back in Copper Cove."

"Me too."

Meow!

"Yes, Jinx," I said, "we know you are too."

CHAPTER 18

Raven and Peyton went home to check in with their families, and I stayed at Aunt Aggie's to help her get the upstairs ready for her guests on Wednesday. Around seven, Chief Baedie called to let Aunt Aggie know she could open her library and clean it. I took that to mean the warrant finally came through, he retrieved the dress, and Barbie was at the station being questioned.

I'd just put the sheets in the washing machine when Grams lumbered into the laundry room grumbling.

"What's up with you?" I asked.

"Glitter and sparkles should be outlawed," she said.

"Are you still vacuuming glitter off the floor?"

"Your aunt put me to work cleaning the library," Grams said. "You don't really notice it until you go to vacuum. I don't know how anyone has any glitter left on their clothes. It seems to have all ended up on the floor."

Something about that statement made me pause.

"Did you clean the chair where Temperance was murdered?" I asked.

Grams shuddered. "Yes. I don't know why Aggie just doesn't throw it away. No one is ever going to want to sit on it again."

"Was there a lot of glitter on the chair?"

"Tons!" Grams exclaimed. "Mostly on the ground, but some in the chair. And what's shocking is that I'm sure they gathered some of it for evidence, and there was still so much left behind."

"I just put the sheets in the washer," I said. "I'm going to run to the apothecary and grab the elderberry syrup for Beatrice."

"Take my car," Grams offered.

Meow! Meow!

"Not this time, buddy," I said. "You stay here and watch over everyone."

Meooooow!

I rolled my eyes. "I said no. End of story."

I didn't drive very often, so I was a nervous wreck when I got behind the wheel of a car. Luckily the town pretty much shuts down after six, so there weren't any cars in front of the apothecary, and I didn't have to parallel park. I ran inside and grabbed the elderberry syrup off the shelf. As I locked the front door, the question that had been bothering me all night about the glitter finally broke through.

Grabbing my phone, I dialed Peyton and then Raven, telling them I was headed to Beatrice's house, and I needed them to come with me. After I nabbed them from their houses, I did a quick drive-by at the diner to make sure Thomas' car was there.

It was.

"Are you sure about this?" Peyton asked as I pulled Grams' car into Beatrice's driveway. "I mean, we all but offered Barbie up on a platter to Chief Baedie."

"Mom was on the phone with Chief Baedie when I left," Raven said. "I'm sure it's about Barbie and Temperance's murder."

"I'm not sure about anything," I said. "But this *feels* right. Grams was going on and on about the amount of glitter

112

found not only on the library floor, but in the actual *chair* Temperance was found in. If there was that much glitter, that meant there had to be a struggle, which explains how Temperance got some of the glitter on her body and under her nails. But when Raven and I looked at the dress upstairs in Barbie's closet, the only thing wrong with it was the missing rhinestone. The glitter in the veins running throughout the dress was all still intact. It doesn't make sense that there's that much glitter in the chair and still on Barbie's dress."

"So your plan is to just mosey in there and ask Beatrice to see the Christmas sweater she wore to the party?" Raven asked.

I shrugged. "Something like that. We'll just ask to see the sweater. Heck, if she's still as sick as she was yesterday, we could just go look for ourselves and she'd never know. She's so out of it."

"And what exactly are we looking for?" Peyton asked.

"If there was a struggle of any kind," I said, "I'm guessing the front of Beatrice's sweater will be glitter free."

"Let's get this ball into motion," Raven said.

I knocked on the door, but Beatrice didn't answer. Ringing the doorbell, I peered through the side window to see if she was around. I saw her stagger to the front door.

"I think she's worse," I said as the front door opened.

Beatrice Baskins looked worse than death if that was possible. Her skin was sallower than it was yesterday, her sweat-soaked hair was stuck to her skull, her eyes were sunken into her face, and she could barely stand on her own two feet.

I reached out, caught her before she fell, and stepped inside the house.

"Beatrice," I said, "why isn't Thomas here taking care of you?"

Beatrice motioned for me to move her into the kitchen. "He'll be here shortly. He needed to be at the diner for the dinner rush, but then he's coming home. He left me veggie broth to drink until he gets back."

Her voice was barely above a whisper. I had a sneaky suspicion that she was going to need more than elderberry syrup to make her feel better.

"What did the doctor tell you?" I asked as I gently lowered her to the kitchen table.

"He thinks it's the flu. Vomiting, diarrhea, fever, exhaustion, dehydration."

I frowned. "That sounds like more than just the flu."

"Thomas is coming home. He's made me veggie broth."

"Beatrice," Raven said, "that Christmas sweater you wore to the party the other night, I sure did like it. Do you know where you got it?"

Beatrice frowned and wiped at the sweat on her forehead. "The sweater? No."

"Do you think I could look at the tag so I could tell?" Raven asked.

"Upstairs," Beatrice whispered. "I can't make it."

"It's okay," Raven said quickly. "I'll go up and look. Which room?"

"First door...on right."

Raven dashed out of the kitchen, and Peyton and I watched silently as Beatrice lifted a shaking hand to her mouth. The soup spilled back into the bowl.

"Let me put that in a cup for you," Peyton said.

As Peyton opened up cupboards looking for a mug, I studied Beatrice. I knew if I got a confession from her, it probably wouldn't hold up because she was so loopy she'd probably say anything. But I had to try.

"Why did you kill Temperance?" I asked.

"Because I knew as long as she was still alive, Thomas would always love her and not me."

My mouth dropped open. I hadn't really expected her to tell me. Peyton said nothing, just poured the soup into the mug.

"Try drinking it from the cup," Peyton said.

How Peyton could be so calm, I had no idea.

Beatrice took a sip of the soup and then started to gag. Peyton ran to the counter, grabbed a bowl, and held it under Beatrice's mouth. When she finished, Beatrice rested her face in her hands while Peyton set the bowl aside.

"So after you left the conservatory," I said, "where did you really go?"

"I went to the bathroom to fix my face," Beatrice panted. "But on the way there, I saw Temperance slip inside the library. I decided to confront her, and I was almost to the library when that dimwit Barbie came sashaying up the hallway." Beatrice lifted her head and stared at me with glassy eyes. "I turned away and pretended not to see her. I was going to enter the library, but I heard arguing. I cracked open the door, and I saw Temperance push Barbie out the

French doors and into the side yard. I closed the door and waited to see what would happen. After a few minutes, I heard the other door close. I waited for them to come out. When no one did, I looked around to make sure no one was paying attention, and slipped into the room."

With a cry, Beatrice clutched her stomach and doubled over in agonizing pain. I felt sorry for her, but I had to know the rest of the story.

"And then what? You walked over to where Temperance was, saw the scarf hanging on the peg, and..."

"And thought I'd been given a gift from above. I thought why not?" Beatrice moaned. "Here was my chance to get rid of the woman who would always stand in the way of my true happiness. And the scarf was right there. It was perfect."

"Only you weren't expecting Temperance to put up such a fight, were you?" I asked.

"No. She looked up at me from the chair where she was reading. Her neck exposed to me." Beatrice wheezed in a pitiful laugh. "She was pretty scrappy for a rich broad. Didn't think she had it in her."

Once again Beatrice turned green and started to gag. Luckily she didn't seem to have anything left in her to come out. She rested her head on the table and moaned.

"Didn't you worry about your sweater?" I asked. "Surely you had to know it was ruined and you still had to get out of the house?"

"Not really," she whispered. "No one would ever notice but Thomas. If he cared to look."

"Do you have any ginger ale or anything?" I asked.

"Refrigerator," Beatrice gasped.

I opened the refrigerator and was about to have Peyton dial 911 and get Beatrice to a hospital when I noticed something in the refrigerator that made my blood turn to ice.

"Beatrice? Why do you have Death Cap mushrooms in your refrigerator?"

"What?" Beatrice tried to focus on me, but she became violently ill again. Unfortunately, there wasn't anything handy for her to get sick in.

"They're poisonous?" Peyton asked, moving away from Beatrice.

"Very," I said. "I read in one of Grams' books it doesn't even take a full mushroom cap to kill someone. Just two years ago down around San Francisco, something like fifteen people were sick from eating the mushrooms. I'm talking like they had to have liver transplants. There have been countless deaths all over the world linked to this mushroom."

"How can you tell it's a Death Cap mushroom?" Peyton asked.

"Greenish tint to it," I bent down and sniffed. "Slight ammonia smell. It's poisonous."

"But this doesn't make any sense," Peyton said. "I thought you said *Beatrice* was the killer. Why would she now be poisoning herself?"

Movement had me looking up in the kitchen archway.

"She's not," I said.

A slow clap echoed off the high ceilings as Thomas Baskins swaggered into the room. "I see you have a little of your grandma's abilities in you."

"Enough to know you're killing Beatrice," I countered.

"I don't understand," Peyton said. "I thought Beatrice killed Temperance?"

"She did," Thomas said. "And for that, I'm killing her."

"The mushrooms aren't in season," I said. "How did you come across one so quickly?"

Thomas smiled and walked to the counter. His eyes flickered over to Beatrice and he grimaced. "I knew her death would be slow, but this is just torturous to have to deal with."

"Where?" I demanded.

"I've been dabbling in horticulture for a while now," he said. "You'd be amazed at what you can grow and keep alive in the right temperatures."

"And so you've been growing them to feed Beatrice one day?" Peyton asked.

"No. I originally thought I'd kill Temperance. Pay her back for the pain and humiliation she caused me when she dumped me." He shook his head. "God I loved that woman." His eyes flashed with rage. "Or maybe I thought to feed it to Granger eventually. Not only has he been stealing my customers, but he stole my woman."

"You were already married!" I cried.

Thomas shrugged.

"But instead you used it on Beatrice," Peyton said.

"I had one cultivating already, and so I figured now was the perfect time after what she did. I just sliced off a tiny bit here and there so there'd be no detection. The morning after the murder, I made an omelet for Beatrice's breakfast. Symptoms can show as soon as six hours or so. By the time you girls stopped by, she was already dying."

"And then you gave it to her in the vegetable broth?" I asked.

"Yes. Again, just a tiny sliver. Then I took her to see the doctor. Played the concerned husband." He glared over at Beatrice, but she was too far gone to see. "I wasn't going to feed her any more, just wait another week for the poison to do its work. It's already attacked her liver and kidneys. The damage is irreversible. She's all but a walking corpse."

"My gosh!" I gasped. "You're a horrible monster!"

I looked up and saw Raven in the doorway. Putting her finger to her lips, she motioned for me to not give her away. Which was hard to do, because Jinx was sitting at her feet! There was no way he should be here. I'd left him at home!

"Why, Thomas?" Beatrice gasped out. "I loved you."

"Why? *Why?*" Thomas screamed as he whipped out a gun from his pocket. "Because you killed the only woman I'd ever love!" Thomas' crazed eyes met mine. "Where's the other one? The freaky looking girl with the purple hair and nose ring?"

"It's just me and Peyton," I said. "Raven stayed home."

Meow! Meow!

Thomas whirled and my heart dropped as Jinx appeared in the doorway. "What's a cat doing in here? I'm allergic!"

Thomas bolted forward, lifted the gun, and I screamed for Jinx to run. But instead of running, Jinx gave me a wink and swished his tail behind him. Tiny black spots danced over my vision, and I was sure I was about to faint...when Raven suddenly stepped into the doorway, the *A Christmas*

Story lamp in her hand. Lifting the lamp, she swung at Thomas like a candy-starved kid taking on a piñata.

One swing and Thomas was on the ground.

Bolting into action, Peyton and I ran for Thomas as Raven kicked the gun into the living room. I plopped down on him as hard as I could...feeling good with myself when I heard him grunt and the air leave his body.

"Someone should probably call—"

I didn't even finish the sentence. Sirens blared from outside, and a couple seconds later the door burst open and Chief Baedie and two policemen piled in.

"I already took care of that," Raven said.

CHAPTER 19

"Hurry, Brynn," Peyton said as we crossed the street to Aunt Aggie's house.

Aunt Aggie was having an intimate New Year's Eve party, and Peyton, Raven, and I were excited to finally meet Chef Granger's grandson. He'd moved to Copper Cove the day before, and tonight he and his dad were coming to the party.

Brandon Powell waved at us from Aunt Aggie's porch. He and Peyton had been spending a few hours together during the Christmas break, and I was thrilled to see Peyton happy. It had been a rough week and a half around town.

Beatrice Baskins had died on the way to the hospital. When I phoned Grams and told her what Beatrice had consumed, she immediately got on the phone with the doctor and begged him to give Beatrice an intravenous milk thistle injection to try and counter the poison, but it didn't do any good in the end. Beatrice's organs had already shut down. Thomas' arrest went from attempted murder to murder.

I'd also heard through the grapevine that Barbie and Mitzi had moved out of the Clairmont mansion. Evidently, even though the rhinestone could be traced back to Barbie, it was just one of those things. It really did just accidentally fall off. That all came straight from Brandon. It seems Percy had paid them a visit a day before Christmas, and after he told them about Barbie, he said their debt was wiped clean. They owed nothing in back rent and they could continue to live in the house.

"It's about time you guys were getting here," Brandon teased. "I was almost ready to give up and go inside."

"Did you meet Chef Granger's grandson yet?" I asked.

"Nope," Brandon said. "They're already here. I wanted to wait for you guys."

"Let's do this," I said.

I really wanted to like the grandson. After all, Aunt Aggie was now officially seeing Chef Granger, so in a way, if things worked out, this guy could end up being around a lot.

"Over here," Grams waved from the fireplace.

Henley handed us each a flute of sparkling apple juice as Jinx nudged my leg. I bent down to give him some love when Chef Granger walked into the room.

"Everyone," he said, "I'd like to introduce you to my son and grandson."

I looked up from my crouched position on the floor and my mouth dropped open. Chef Granger's grandson was hot enough to melt cold butter.

Recipes:

Maddy and I love making soaps and scrubs. Since this is a holiday story, we are going to share our favorite holiday three-pack gift set you can put in a basket and give away: Peppermint soap, Peppermint hand scrub, and Peppermint lip scrub.

Peppermint Glycerin Soap

Materials:
1 lb Clear Glycerin (Amazon)
1-2 Drops Red Soap Colorant (Amazon)
3-4 Drops Peppermint Essential Oil
Soap Molds (Hobby Lobby/Amazon)
Knife
2 cup Measuring Glass with spout
Rubbing alcohol
Cling Wrap

Assemble:
1) Cut your glycerin into cubes.
2) Put cubes in glass measuring cup.
3) Microwave 20 second intervals until melted. Do not over melt or you will get foam.
4) Add red colorant and peppermint scent.
5) Carefully pour glycerin into the molds, being careful not to pour too quickly. You don't want air bubbles.

6) If you have bubbles, lightly spray or brush the rubbing alcohol over top of soap and they should dissipate.
7) Let sit on counter for about 3 hours. Check. They should be hard enough to pop out and wrap in cling wrap. Store in closet.
8) Should make 8-10 soaps.

Peppermint Sugar Scrub for Hands

We are doing the Peppermint scent here, but orange works great for holiday smell, also!

Materials:
1/2 Cup Granulated Sugar
2 Tablespoons Liquid Coconut Oil (We used organic)
8-10 Drops Peppermint Essential Oil
Air-tight glass container (Hobby Lobby)
Large glass bowl
Spoon

1) Simply put the first three ingredients in the glass bowl and stir, making sure to mix everything well.
2) Store in the air-tight glass container.

Peppermint Lip Scrub

Materials:
1 Tsp Coconut Oil (we used Organic)
1 Tsp Honey
1 ½ Tsp Sugar
3 Drops Peppermint Essential Oil
Small air-tight glass container (Hobby Lobby)

Mix all the ingredients together and put in a clear glass jar. Rub on lips, then leave the scrub on for a minute or two before wiping off with a damp towel.

Have you read the Sullivan Sisters Mysteries with bookstore/bar owner Jaycee Sullivan and her boozy baker sister, Jax? If not, now is the time to try it for only $0.99 or FREE on Kindle Unlimited! Just click here!! https://www.amazon.com/dp/B01KECDAOQ

ABOUT THE AUTHOR

Jenna writes in the genres of cozy/paranormal cozy/ romantic comedy. Her humorous characters and stories revolve around over-the-top family members, creative murders, and there's always a positive element of the military in her stories. Jenna currently lives in Missouri with her fiancé, step-daughter, Nova Scotia duck tolling retriever dog, Brownie, and her tuxedo-cat, Whiskey. She is a former court reporter turned educator turned full-time writer. She has a Master's degree in Special Education, and an Education Specialist degree in Curriculum and Instruction. She also spent twelve years in full-time ministry.

When she's not writing, Jenna likes to attend beer and wine tastings, go antiquing, visit craft festivals, and spend time with her family and friends. Check out her website at http://www.jennastjames.com/. Don't forget to sign up for the newsletter so you can keep up with the latest releases! You can also friend request her on Facebook at jennastjamesauthor/ or catch her on Instagram at authorjennastjames.

Made in the USA
Columbia, SC
15 December 2019

84953257R00070